Pr[

"A gothic tale of love and betrayal, of faith and temptation, and of violence under the guise of piety."
ELIZABETH BRUCE, AUTHOR OF *AND SILENT LEFT THE PLACE*

"This lyrical, thoughtful work ponders good and evil,
love and betrayal, and what it means to be human. It's
also an old-school gothic novel that has a lot of fun
with the form and is packed with horror, romance,
and beautifully overwrought emotion."
NORAH VAWTER, AUTHOR AND EDITOR

"Delivers everything that a fan of gothic fiction could
want—a crumbling, haunted abbey, an endangered
heroine, supernatural intervention, unrelenting
suspense... will have you guessing until the end."
EDWARD BELFAR, AUTHOR OF THE INDEPENDENT PRESS
AWARD WINNING NOVEL *A VERY INNOCENT MAN*

About the Author

Mike Maggio's publication credits include fiction, poetry, travel and reviews in many local, national and international publications including *Potomac Review, The L.A. Weekly, The Washington CityPaper*, and *The Washington Independent Review of Books*. His full-length publications include a novel, *The Wizard and the White House*, a novella, *The Appointment*, and a collection of short stories, *Letters from Inside*. His latest collection of poetry, *Let's Call It Paradise*, won the International Book Award for Contemporary Poetry in 2024.

www.mikemaggio.net

Woman

in the

Abbey

Mike Maggio

www.vineleavespress.com

Cover design by Jessica Bell
Interior design by Amie McCracken

for Drew

Chapter 1

I won't tell you my story from the beginning. At least, not that cursed beginning which has been related countless times and from which I can never escape. For I'd have to go back to a time that had no real origin. An indeterminate inception filled with iniquity and fraught with injustice, despite the guise of righteousness you have been led to believe.

The genesis, shall we say, of my fiery ruin.

No, I will not recount the perdition into which I was cast. The sulfurous caverns from which I emerge. The dark, blazing chambers to which I must constantly return. Nor will I ask for pity. I won't give *him* that satisfaction. For I have borne *his* sting ever since. Will bear it forever and more.

Besides: this is not my story. Not really. Though, perhaps, it will somehow resemble that despicable tale. No, this is a story involving others. *About* others. And in some ways, it might be about you. For it's a story entailing sin and immorality, things, I am certain, you are familiar with. A story about faith and doubt and the evil that lies within, waiting to disgorge. You understand, don't you? Or at least you will, when all is said and done.

Our story, then, happened much later than mine. Yet, like mine, it has no recognizable beginning and no endurable end. Instead, it repeats itself in various ways, over and over and over. It runs its course with no lasting resolution, though the particulars may vary. The era. The place. The individuals involved. Sometimes, there's a vengeful woman. Sometimes, a man on the precipice of desperation. Often, there are children involved. Innocent children, caught up in events beyond their control. Beyond their ability to fight back. To defend themselves. But ultimately, the story is the same. As if it were a template for mankind's woes. And though it ends tragically—for the individuals involved, at least—it soon resumes—resurrects, shall we say?—in another shape and form.

Unlike mine. Mine never changes. Mine has no end. Mine simply is.

But let's forget about all that. I have no need for bitterness, as I burrow here in this mournful citadel of sin. Nor do I mean to petition your sympathy. Or even, to demand a modicum of mercy. I am here simply to tell you a story. A melancholy story, to be sure. To lure you into its sordid details. To tempt you into believing something you do not wish to acknowledge. A story about individuals you will no doubt recognize. Some with whom you will surely sympathize. Others whom you will likely abhor. Some, perhaps, who will test your limits for tolerance. But in the end, when all is said and done, it won't really matter. I'll relate and you'll listen— hungrily, perhaps, greedily. You'll return, over and over. Pore over each foul detail. Review each macabre incident. Despite your protests. Despite your claims of virtue and righteousness. And, yes: even justice.

And the rest, shall we say, will be left to destiny.

Chapter 2

I'll start with Father Francesco, a troubled monk, rotund in stature, humble by nature, with just a touch of timidity, embroiled in the throes of inner uncertainty. Lying in his bed as a violent storm rages outside his meager cell. As the abbey, where he has come to spend eternity, barely endures each fierce squall. As the dormitory, where solace evades his every fervent prayer, trembles from the vicious lashes of the howling wind.

Like most who ended up here, Father Francesco yearned to forget, for the abbey had beckoned him with its illusion of solitude, with the temptation of renunciation and forgiveness—with the lure of the soothing waters of Lethe. Just as it had seduced, throughout the ages, the countless wretched men and women who found their way to its portals in their own hour of distress.

Here, secluded within it towering walls, he took his daily bread—what scanty scraps there were—just as the others did—monks and nuns, anointed alike into a life of sheer austerity. A life where abnegation was meant to purge the shameful sins of their past. Every day, he toiled in silence, urgently praying at each appointed hour. Each night, he attempted to cleanse himself of the dark memories that forever shrouded his soul. His prayers were frantic—filled with dread—and he could never seem to forget whatever sinful deeds he had at one time committed. Deeds that loomed every minute like the crimson-stained glass that cast its shadow over the abbey's somber chapel. Dire deeds that forever tarnished his conscience with their indelible tinge.

I, too, inhabited the abbey. Cloaked in obscurity, I lived, if that be the right word, among them—the newly christened monks and nuns—unseen, though very much a part of their lives. And yet their attempts at reverence were a far cry from my ungodly nature. For *he* had not wished me to be like them: god-fearing and upright. Willing to grovel, night and day. And I complied. Not willingly. But compliance does not require the willingness of the victim.

Each day, I accompanied them, an invisible shadow, as they went about their affairs, though they pretended to be unaware. Each moment, I tempted them as they toiled, seduced them as they chanted, beguiled them with deeds more tantalizing so as to assuage their fiery anguish. I'd whisper notions into their ears—intoxicating suggestions—alluring distractions in an otherwise wearisome place—as they meditated in private or passed each other in silence. I'd accompany them, in their solitude, as they trod the paths of the cold, stone hallways, ready to suggest a more inviting detour. And each night, as the moon melted into the restive clouds and they lay uneasy in their comfortless beds, questioning the straight and narrow and yearning, secretly, for a life beyond those somber, austere walls, I'd attend to their sorrows, provide a sliver of solace as they wrought their uncertainties into a maze of disquiet. And I would try, unfeigned, to ease their souls with thoughts less celestial, more—shall we say?—down to earth. For the call of the flesh is something not so easily tamed.

Father Francesco knew of my presence. They all knew, though they pretended otherwise. Though they avoided me as one avoids a leper or an unfortunate plague-stricken soul. In vain, they strove to resist my entreaties. Just as they had done in the past. Just as *you* have done from time to time. Yet, when they least expected, I would stand beside them—as their hands were folded in prayer or as they chanted psalms or read from their breviaries—and quietly tempt them with things more palpable. More gratifying. More profane. Still, they would not see—refused to acknowledge my bid for companionship—no matter how I offered solace. And yet, I persisted. I slithered my way into their most fervent thoughts, tainted each supplication, deflected each ardent appeal for forgiveness. Resistance was their only recourse and sleep their only escape. For in those murky realms of slumber, reality disappears and even the worst deeds—the most ardent desires—can sometimes be laid to rest. Temporarily, at least.

Or perhaps not.

For on this stormy night, as our story commences and a fateful wind wails through the murky darkness, Father Francesco lies in his bed, shrouded in dreams—twisted dreams from which he cannot escape. Dreams that no man could possibly abide. He tosses and turns. He wrestles with the unknown. He struggles to escape from this, his eternal nightmare—a nightmare for which no devil's bargain can ever be made.

Chapter 3

As Father Francesco shrank into his nightmares, a stark chill devoured what little comfort his meager fireplace had to offer. Hidden among the burning embers, I watched as he squirmed beneath his flimsy cowl, impotent against the demons that had come to afflict him. Warming my sallow flesh in the soothing flames, I waited for an opportunity—an opening—to ease his troubled mind, to offer counsel in his moment of distress, to help appease the relentless apparitions and swaddle him in a cocoon of delusion until his time of reckoning would at last arrive. For it is in those uncertain hours of desperation that one is most susceptible to surrender.

Soon, the clock commenced its midnight knell, echoing through the darkness like the faint cries of a ghost condemned to its anxious fate, until the pendulum ceased its eternal ticking—stopped cold at the eleventh stroke—and Father Francesco awoke with a violent jolt.

Terrified, he opened his eyes and wiped his brow and stared through the miasma of slumber at the darkness that cloaked him. The moon cast an uneasy eye upon the wall as the ancient abbey groaned against the ruthless wind. Outside, the trees moaned, and the yelp of a frightened animal pierced the vicious din.

And then, there arose a sound that beckoned him like a siren—a faint cry, barely audible through the storm's exquisite thunder.

Father Francesco leaned forward. His heart quaked, and he broke out into a sudden sweat, for it was a sound he understood intimately, as one comes to know the groaning of the gallows or the distinct rattle of death's final call.

Reaching for the rosary buried within his flimsy cowl, he jumped up and rushed from his cell, hastening through the cold corridors as the hands of time pressed against each restive step. At each turn, he muttered supplications and begged for guidance. At each vacant doorway, he prayed for mercy, until he came to a hidden portal that opened up to the barren courtyard and the uncertainty that lay beyond. Squalls of leaves swirled around him like jinn as he proceeded along the narrow pathway. Apprehensive, he approached the iron gateway that separated the dead from the living, and prayed, once again, for guidance—*his* guidance. For beyond that forbidden entrance, buried deep within the abbey's musty bowels, lay the gruesome secrets that no living soul wished to concede—no one, at least, who had not had the privilege of consorting with me.

Slowly, he descended down the broken stone steps, down to the caverns where the dead awaited, as the faint cry lured him further into his uncertain destiny. Blindly traversing the dark corridors, he stumbled over bones and mummified limbs, until he reached the chamber from which the desperate cries emerged—a chamber no man of flesh and blood had wish to enter.

And then, through the thick atmosphere came, once again, that feeble sound—a wailing so hopeless, so despondent that Father Francesco could do nothing but conjure once more a plea for mercy. Muttering words blasphemous to my ears, he attempted the sign of the cross and clutched the beads dangling from his trembling hand until he found the strength to open the door to that wretched chamber. Torches blazed from the stone walls and blinded his vision, but there was no need to see, for he knew very well the dark shadow that materialized before his eyes, knew, as well, the shrill voice that filled his unwilling ears.

"Vile woman! Let the evil pass from your wicked flesh!"

Tall and gaunt and dressed in a stiff, black habit, Sister Lucretia, the Mother Superior of that ill-fated abbey, loomed like an inquisitor over her victim—an unfortunate woman whose time had come and whose cries of anguish were those that had summoned Father Francesco from his unsettling dreams. Barely clothed, she lay on the stone sepulcher that had become her birthing bed, her legs splayed and her arms bound in chains. Beside her, crouched like a swarm of black spiders, a horde of nuns carried out the pitiless commands of their cruel cloistress.

"Peace be upon you, Father," Sister Lucretia said, turning her gaze.

"What, in the name of God—"

"We are helping this woman through her trial, Father," she answered. "We are handling this as God wishes."

"God does not demand such cruelty. God is merciful!"

Sister Lucretia reached for the rosary pinned to her starched habit and gripped the bare crucifix with the tip of her withered fingers. Her eye glowed with infernal zeal, and she bore into Father Francesco's soul and slowly tapped her foot until he lowered his gaze. Satisfied, she turned to her keep.

"More hot water!" she commanded.

"Let me be, in God's name!"

"In God's name, woman!? Do you now call on God when you have so shamelessly abandoned Him? When it is now too late to ask for forgiveness? When you should have prayed for His guidance before committing your wicked deed? You must release the child so we can destroy it and you can be cleansed of your sins."

Stooping down, she yanked the woman by her hair and shoved her severe face into hers.

"It is evil, like its father. Like the act which led to its creation. Like the woman who bears it. We cannot let it stain the walls of our sacred dwelling!"

"You cannot," the woman cried. "I will not let you!"

"You have no choice," Sister Lucretia said, releasing her grip. "Evil must be destroyed. That is our sacred mission."

"Sister Lucretia," Father Francesco demanded. "I will not allow you to defile the abbey in this way."

"Defile? Defile, Father Francesco? Am I to understand that you condone this woman's behavior?"

"I demand that you show mercy!"

"Very well," she answered. "I understand. Bring the hot oil," she commanded. "Boiling, scalding oil."

"Yes, Mother Superior."

And Father Francesco beheld the crime. Beheld, with a trembling eye and an unsettled soul, the iniquity that had befallen that abbey from the days before his arrival, witnessed the wickedness that had repeated itself over and over throughout the centuries. He knew full well what he had to do, knew that in doing so he would have to confront me, knew that weakness would overcome and ultimately succeed. Grasping his beads, he rushed out of that lugubrious chamber and disappeared down the moribund corridors, disappeared into the haunted hallways of an abbey from which he knew there was no palpable escape.

Chapter 4

Throughout my mission—my unwavering devotion to mankind—I have been known to assist all breed of individuals—kings and queens struggling with their tenuous rule or with their fickle minions; abandoned children, wandering in the wilderness, cut off from parents and siblings, surviving only on wild berries and what streams they might stumble upon; men whose lives have reached a sudden juncture from which there is no return; distressed damsels seeking only rescue and solace.

I have a reputation—a responsibility, shall we say? For I give advice—unsolicited guidance—and offer the most relevant respite and even, at times, a convenient way out. I suggest a means of deliverance to the abandoned, to those who, in the midst of their most irreversible turns of fortune, crave patronage and aid at just about any cost. And when they have cried out in desperation and have received only the hollowest echo of their own voice in return, when they have prayed fiercely and supplicated in vain, burnished their most cherished beads until, at last, they have run out of hope, I come to their aid, often unbeknownst to them, though they secretly, desperately have yearned for my assistance all along.

It's not as if I seek out such individuals. Often, they come to me, in those moments when their very survival depends on some unattainable resolution. And, as I loathe to see men suffer—as my heart swells with a painful poignancy as they hunger for comfort and salvation, I ultimately succumb, demanding little up front, though payment, as we all know, always gets settled in the end. For one has a sense of obligation—a responsibility, don't you think?—that recompense is due for services rendered. You've been there before, haven't you? And when the time comes to remit, one pays up, willingly or not.

Such were the circumstances that very night, as poor, helpless Perdita—for that was that unfortunate woman's name—endured the fiery zeal of Sister Lucretia, as that coterie of nuns participated, willingly or not, in her fervent inquisition, pinning Perdita down as she squirmed in agony. And as Father Francesco struggled with his failure to come to her rescue, she invoked *his* name over and over but was answered merely by a blaring echo of silence—a silence interrupted only by the clamor of Sister Lucretia's wicked ministrations and of her band of iniquitous assistants who held Perdita captive as they applied all means to rid her of her wicked burden, to purge her of sin and evil, to assure that retribution was paid as retribution deserved.

Thrashing about in labor and succumbing pitifully to her torture, Perdita cried out in vain for relief and mercy, shouted prayers that fell futilely on ever-deaf ears, then took to cursing her persistent persecutors, all from the instinct of survival for herself and her unborn child. I could hardly bear it—watching that sweet suffering, hearing the utter futility of her cries, witnessing the indifference—the cruelty—exhibited by those sworn to holiness—the cold, callous attitude toward the anguish of one in need. Knowing that she yearned for salvation from that untenable situation, and unable, any longer, to temper my sorrow, I stepped in.

It was a difficult situation, as they typically tend to be, for I had to conceal myself, hide my form and identity from those with whom I had sometimes consorted. It required cunning, skill, an ability to make use of the tools at hand. Yet, faced with this challenge, I immediately set to work.

I assessed the chamber, took note of the torches that burned atop their unsteady sconces, listened to the wind howling above. And I stared at that cauldron of boiling oil, sitting precariously on its nest of flames, and noted that Perdita was protected by the stone crypt on which she was held captive.

Catacombs are notorious for being cold and drafty. Along with a dank chill that cuts through the bones—of those, at least, who are among the living—there sometimes comes an abrupt burst of wind, a sudden gust, brief yet noticeable, that whistles its eerie cry through those dark shafts and often keeps away grave robbers, fearing ghosts and goblins and other such conjured creatures. From where these chilly currents of air emanate is something best left for scientists and learned men to discern. Perhaps it comes through tunnels dug by beasts to nest and gather warmth. Or, maybe, it's the remnant gasps of those buried in those subterranean chambers, rising up in sudden bouts of anxiousness as they come to grips with their uncertain eternity.

In our case, as you will recall, the winds were blowing furiously up above, and the fading gasps of those sudden squalls, entering through such caverns as were made by man and beast, provided the perfect access for their unpredictable blasts. The torches, already struggling to stay alive, flickered wildly as a sudden gasp of wind blew through the passageways of those ancient tombs, and soon the chamber was engulfed in darkness, a darkness filled with ghostly howls that were enough to raise the hairs on the shrouded bodies of those wicked nuns. Suddenly, the vault was swallowed in silence, interrupted only by the wailing of the wind and the grating of Perdita's heavy chains against the stone tomb upon which she lay.

The holy nuns, Sister Lucretia included, mumbled among themselves—sputters of prayers and words of apprehension and distress—and then, as the door to that chamber suddenly flew open with a furious clang that echoed through the dark vault, a sliver of light appeared, and the nuns abandoned their stations and scurried, as quickly as their cumbersome habits and the darkness would allow. As they tried desperately to run out of that chamber and toward the gloomy corridors, their faces as white as the bones they traversed, their bodies trembling from fear, that boiling cauldron tipped over, spilling its fiery contents, and engulfed those sorry nuns in its burning hunger, leaving poor Perdita alone in the unhallowed darkness.

Alas, that was all I could do for poor Perdita, though, till now, she has never forgotten my kindness. But duty called, and I was forced to depart those dire dungeons to come to the aid of yet another forlorn creature.

Chapter 5

Many years later—decades, centuries, perhaps, for such is time that it has no distinctive measure—I ascended those drafty crypts to come to the aid of yet another desperate damsel: a beautiful young woman whose name was Graziella and who, early one wintry morning, came rushing through the shadows, scrambling through brush and dead briar, tripping over gnarled tree stubs and scattered limbs, all the while clenching tightly around her slender neck a loose black cape in which she was fully cloaked.

She was fleeing from some mundane affair—the kind that afflicts men and women time and time again—an affair she had unwittingly become entangled in, or so she reasoned—one so shameful, so profane, that she believed she had no choice but to run away. Now, alone in the cold, lonely forest, she battled both dread and memory as she ran whichever way she could, sensing, all along, that she was being pursued. And though she could not determine, through the remnants of the frightful night, who—or what—it was that might be chasing her, she could clearly hear, echoing in the near distance, the crush of footsteps against the cold forest floor. Against all reason, she prayed to *him*—prayed that it might be a wild animal, though, surely, she thought, it would have pounced on her by now, and not some supernatural denizen of the forest—a troll or some evil imp—conjured up in the far reaches of her traumatized mind. Whatever it was, she could feel its presence and, arousing my jealousy and provoking my ire, she implored *him*, most desperately, to deliver escape before it set its fiendish clutches on her tender body.

But I'm taunting you. Refusing to say who or what she was running away from. And, you, I trust, are enjoying it. For, let's face it: you are tantalized by such scenes. The mental anguish. The possibility of bodily harm. The potential for violence and violation. Mesmerized, you lie snug in your bed or curled up in your armchair as a storm suddenly brews. The thunder thickens and the lights flicker. Startled, you look up as a loud rumble rattles the house—rattles your most startled soul. It's a delicious sort of delight, isn't it? Manifested by Graziella's helplessness and your sheer sense of terror. And yet, you remain safely ensconced in your little world. Safe in the hopes that Graziella will escape all harm. For she is, after all, the heroine of this little tale.

As you burrow into your fear—terrified for yourself, though why, you cannot say—our ill-fated heroine hastens through the mist, attempts to conceal herself beneath the shadows of the morning twilight, hiding wherever she can—behind trees, beneath bushes—as the moon races through the scattered clouds and reveals drifts of dead leaves, knots of tangled branches—as it unveils each tenuous hiding place in the wake of its erratic path. Terrified, she tears through the haunted forest while her pursuer, obscured by the waning darkness, stalks her from behind. And you, meanwhile, remain curled up in anxiety—squirming, trembling, enjoying, in some perverse way, Graziella's precarious dilemma.

But let me continue.

As Graziella rushed through the darkness, and the snap of broken branches cut through the silence, the distant howl of a lonely wolf rose up against the impending dawn. A night owl, seeking solace in that baleful forest, moaned a melancholy hoot. Graziella, trembling at each dampened echo, took comfort in their cries—if comfort can be had when one's life feels so imperiled—as if they were harbingers of deliverance, or as if, in their mournful manifestations, she was assured that life—her life—would somehow prevail. Consoled by the unsettled wilderness, she suppressed her fear and sought sanctuary from her shadowy pursuer, beseeching *him*, yet again, from the depths of her terror, that she might be delivered from harm.

At last, peering through the thick blanket of fog that smothered the forest, she spotted the ghostly outline of a refuge hovering in the distance. It was, as she would soon come to know, an abbey—the same abbey you have already become acquainted with—and she pushed forward, stumbling over rocks and debris, reclaiming her balance and forcing herself to pick up her pace. Her lungs burned and her legs ached as she continued to outrun her mysterious pursuer.

Soon, she reached the iron gate that towered against the abbey's ominous form. Abandoning herself into its cold embrace, she shook it with what strength remained as the sound of muffled footsteps drew ever closer.

Miraculously—if that be the right word, for it was I, after all, who had once again to step in—the gate swung open and Graziella slipped through its cavernous mouth, shutting it with a clang that reverberated through the anxious dawn. Breathless, she ran through the labyrinth of pathways that led to the abbey—pathways dense with weed and dead debris—until she reached the deserted courtyard and the abbey's formidable entrance.

Graziella pounded furiously on the massive door as the footsteps drew nearer and her cries for refuge were swallowed by the morning silence.

Just as she was about to surrender—just as hope itself was about to yield to utter desperation—the door opened and there stood before her, eclipsed in shadow, the silhouette of an old woman dressed in white, clutching a candle in her bony fingers, her wizened face wavering above the feeble light of the flickering flame.

"Who calls at this unholy hour of the morning?"

The old woman gazed at Graziella as if to ascertain who this unfortunate creature might be and how, on this cold, bleak morning, she had arrived like a waif at her uninviting doorstep. Her nightdress billowed against the morning chill, and her eye—for she had but one—pulsed in the candle's tenuous haze. Placing her hand on Graziella's shoulder, she pressed firmly as if to absorb her warmth into her frigid body.

The sound of footsteps broke the old woman's spell, and she immediately released her grip and peered through the thick fog that shrouded the abbey.

"Child," she said, turning to Graziella. "You will die from the cold. Come quickly and warm yourself by the fire."

Seizing Graziella, she dragged her into the darkness of the abbey and gazed anxiously at the impending dawn—gazed and mumbled words that only I could comprehend, firmly shutting that impregnable door.

Chapter 6

How can I tell you of the horror that tore through Graziella's delicate frame as she stepped inside that cold, unwelcoming edifice? What words are there to describe the terror that seized her with its jagged claws as she witnessed the devastation that afflicted that godforsaken abbey?

After millennia of harboring those who had come to confess their most intimate deeds and who failed, in the end, in their feigned attempts at repentance, what had once been a solemn testimony to *him* had been transformed into a ghastly sanctuary dedicated solely to me.

Graziella gazed upon the devastation with a look of dread as a sudden sense of pity reverberated through my blackened soul. I watched as she succumbed—as she realized, now, when it was too late, that the refuge she had sought—the refuge she foolishly believed would serve as her salvation—was no refuge at all. Bathed in the melancholy light of the old woman's quivering candle, she stepped unwillingly into the darkness and wondered if she would ever escape its unrelenting arms.

"What is this place?" she asked.

Her voice trembled and her body shivered in fear.

The old woman did not answer. Instead, she drifted silently down the abbey's abandoned hallways as if she were a ghost floating through the ethers—a fallen spirit condemned to a path she was forced to roam, over and over, one that led to the lifeless chamber that was awaiting her unsuspecting visitor.

Reluctant, Graziella followed, clutching her cloak around her slender neck, and gazed through the blinding darkness upon the ruins that encircled her like a widow's wreath. Her body trembled and her heart shuddered, as if she were entering a death chamber or as if, having once believed in the illusion of redemption, she now realized that there was no flicker of hope in the bleakness that consumed her.

As they wandered through the empty corridors, she detected a dull hissing, as of a snake slithering toward her with its venomous tongue. Her head began to spin, and she felt as if she would suffocate as a thin coil of smoke rose up from the old woman's candle and wound its way around her delicate body. Gasping for air, she leaned against the wall and undid the knot of her weary cloak.

The old woman turned and held the candle up to Graziella's face.

"You are weary," she said. "Soon, you shall rest. A deep, soothing rest."

"What is this place?" Graziella repeated.

The old woman's eye glowed in the darkness.

"It is a place of worship," she said. "A placed where light become darkness. And darkness, light."

She stared into Graziella's eyes. Then she turned and continued her mute journey through the bleak corridors.

I could have told Graziella what that place was. I could have related the wicked deeds that had occurred between its crumbling walls, could have revealed the iniquities that had taken place throughout its long, lugubrious existence: the tortures that had been executed, the agonies that had been endured by those who had made their way to its deceiving portals. I could have told her of the fate that had befallen the old woman—what sins she had committed, what lives she had destroyed, what price she had been forced to pay. But my purpose is not to reveal. It is only when the need arises—when the situation becomes so untenable—when no alternative exists—that I feel compelled to offer counsel.

And so it would be for Graziella. Sweet Graziella.

Through the dreary hallways they passed. Darkness was their only companion and the flickering candle their only guide. The sound of Graziella's footsteps echoed against the silence through which they passed, until, suddenly, there arose a cry that caused Graziella's heart to quake, and the old woman to stop and turn to what was now her keep.

"You should not roam these hallways alone," she said. "They are dark and dangerous. You might stumble. Or worse."

Her voice echoed through the emptiness as she looked upon Graziella with her glassy eye.

What is your name, child?"

"Graziella."

"Graziella," the old woman repeated. "Graziella. A name of gratitude. A name that embodies obedience and submission."

Once again, there came a cry. Then, just as suddenly, it died away.

"Do you pray, Graziella? You must pray, child. Pray for forgiveness. Pray for salvation. Pray until your very last breath. Only then will you be answered."

She stared deep into the darkness and her eye flared above the nimbus of the flickering candle.

"Can you feel it, Graziella? Can you feel His presence?"

Graziella grabbed the ties of her cloak and drew them tight.

"I'm frightened," she said.

The old woman whispered in response, muttered words as elusive as the cries that rose and vanished into the piercing silence until, turning once again, she proceeded down the grim hallway, her white gown billowing in the darkness.

At last, they came to a small room, a cell where those who came before had suffered their grief. The door swung open, and the old woman stepped inside and placed the candle on a small black table.

"You will rest here," she said. "Should you need anything, you may summon me."

She pointed to a small bell, tarnished with age, lying on the dusty mantel above the dim fireplace. Staring into the dying embers, she reached inside her night-dress and withdrew a string of worn beads.

"Take these," the old woman said.

She mumbled beneath her breath, mumbled words only I could comprehend.

"Do not let them go. They will be your only protection."

She peered into Graziella's eyes. Then she turned and disappeared into the blackness.

Chapter 7

Graziella clutched the ancient rosary against her trembling breast. Grasping the worn beads between her fingers, she recited prayers of desperation, and nervously glanced around the bleak cell with a look that would have softened even the most callous of hearts.

The chamber was dark and narrow, bare of any semblance of solace, meant merely to spawn fits of self-abnegation and flares of penance. A meager bed, narrow and rigid, dominated the sparsely furnished room. Lying at its foot was an ancient shroud and, at its head, a shriveled cloth stained with specks of dried blood. In one corner stood an old chest, dark gashes trailing down its worm-eaten side. On top: a mound of dust, a torn breviary and the ragged remains of a book— *his* book—having endured the bouts of one caught up in the seizures of self-doubt. And across the room, in a narrow corner, an ancient fireplace burned, unable or unwilling to instill warmth into that comfortless room.

It was there that I lingered, waiting, yearning, concealed among the sputtering flames, gazing upon

Graziella as she stirred and quaked and clutched those dark beads close to her tender breast.

My heart faltered. I could hardly bear the anguish I sensed erupting within her desperate soul—an inferno of anxiety and terror raging out of control. I yearned to exert my powers, to reach deep inside the pit of my tortured heart to reclaim the feelings that had for so long been forbidden me. I considered rushing to her rescue, to quench the flames that were consuming her, to embrace her with my ungainly wings, to exhort her with words—words to allure and convince, gruff though they might be—though how could one such as her suffer the sound of something so unangelic, so jarring by its very nature? And as my heart, hardened by eternity, coiled into a maelstrom of pity and mercy— yes, even love, for what creature in this world is incapable of such feelings?—she slowly removed the hood that covered her head and, through those wavering flames, I beheld her delicate features—her pearl-white face, as pure as an angel's—as comely as mine had once been!—and a mass of thick black hair that cascaded around her slender shoulders. And those deep, brown eyes—so magnificent, so resplendent, as they brimmed with terror. How could I resist such temptation!

Graziella fingered the worn beads the old woman had given her, ground them with an uncertain anxiety, clung to them with such force so as not to slip away.

And I listened insatiably to her helpless laments, muffled as they were, for I was overcome with a feeling that shocked even me—a sensation that had been denied me during my long, abhorrible existence—a forbidden passion I could no longer control. But at that very moment, as I stirred, restless, in the meager flames that pranced about that pitiful fireplace, as I was about to reveal myself in all my ghastly glory—for I have no illusions, no qualms, about my unsightly appearance—there came a sound from outside the splintered window—a dull, brittle sound like the scraping of sharp claws against stone—and I was forced to remain hidden within the flames, lest I add to the horror that now raised every hair on Graziella's delicate body.

Graziella gripped those useless beads as a dark shadow concealed every ray of the morning light that seeped through the window above her meager bed. And as the infernal scratching grew louder, there came a sudden sound: a sound of wheezing. A sound that turned into panting, and that gradually grew into a deafening howl.

Abandoning the old woman's lifeless beads, Graziella jumped up and seized the small handbell on the table, shaking it with such force that the feeble clapper came crashing down to the ground with a faint thud. Just then, the door swung open, and the old nun appeared like a ghost emerging from the veils of darkness. Graziella approached her with apprehension.

"It is just an animal," the old woman said, quietly closing the door.

She snatched the rusted clapper from the floor and fondled it with her wrinkled hand. Then she glanced at the window before turning her blank gaze back toward Graziella.

"A wild animal," she repeated. "Hungry for its morning meal."

The old woman was dressed in a plain black habit, her head concealed by a formless shroud. In one hand, she held a candle which illuminated her pale face. In the other, she clutched a string of beads that were fastened to the side of her garment—beads which, unlike the ones she had bestowed upon Graziella, were capped with a silver crucifix.

"Come," she said.

She let the beads fall to her side and, as the crucifix dangled precariously before my eyes, she held out her hand and said: "It is time for us to break our fast. To feed our bodies. To feed our wretched souls."

The old woman grasped Graziella's hand with her bony fingers.

"We shall take of that which He has granted. Then we shall pray. Pray for salvation. Pray for protection against the evil that dwells within these unholy walls."

She turned and proceeded down the dark hallway, leading her keep silently through the dim uncertain corridors. And I, imprisoned in the flames at the sight of that vindictive crucifix dangling down the old nun's side, was left only to attend to the strident hissing of her unyielding habit as it dragged against the empty hallways of that derelict abbey and the sound of that wretched cross as it struck the walls with each abrasive thud.

Chapter 8

It wasn't long before I was able to join them, for soon, as the old woman drifted into the darkness, that noxious crucifix turned its loathsome face and buried itself in the bitter folds of Sister Lucretia's stiff habit. And so we continued through the dim corridors—three souls: one undead, one undying and one whose fate had yet to come.

With each step, Graziella's heart clamored like a death knell as if she knew what fate had in store for her, and while she now believed that the old woman was a member of an order dedicated to *his* work, she took no comfort in that revelation. Instead, fear gnawed at her insides like a maggot feeding on flesh—fear that consumed her as she witnessed, once again, the devastation that surrounded her.

I followed from behind, swaddled in blackness, one eye firmly on Graziella, the other cautiously minding the old nun whose capacity for evil I knew quite well. For she was my protégé, and I now feared she would utilize the skills I had instilled in her against an innocent creature—one who had touched my heart like no other mortal throughout eternity. And so I attended every move, noted each syllable, heeded each and every utterance, ready to intervene if needed.

At last, having traversed the bleak hallway and having reached its brim, the old nun paused, turned her pale face toward Graziella and said: "Through this portal, we shall enter. There we shall take of that which is granted. Then we shall give of ourselves. For he that taketh must giveth in return."

The nun's words fell upon Graziella's ears with a heaviness that weighed upon her soul, then faded into the void.

"Come," she said.

Together, they entered the dimly lit room and approached a wooden table whose form slowly emerged through the murky light. Upon its worn surface were two small bowls, each containing a lump of bread, and two red goblets filled with water.

Graziella waited for permission to sit, to swat away the flies, to say grace, to partake of the meager meal that lay before her. But the nun simply studied her in silence as if she wanted nothing more than for her to suffer her hunger.

Hidden in the shadows, I looked on, my heart filled with pity for the one and admiration for the other. For such is my fate: to love where love is not requited, to hate with such intensity that it becomes love in disguise, to sit and watch, to wait and hope, to adore, to despise, knowing fully that the fulfillment of my urgent desire, of my very existence, must, in the end, be denied. Such is the destiny to which I was cast and which I must inevitably endure. Still, I bided my time, as I have throughout eternity, for one must never relent, no matter the obstacle, no matter how indelibly one's fortune is branded upon one's soul. One must believe, always, despite the sentence, despite the hopelessness of one's existence, for reprieve must, in the end, somewhere reside, must somehow exist beyond that elusive horizon.

At last, the old nun broke her silence.

"Remember, my child. Solemnity. Deprivation. Abstention. These are the keys to salvation. When there is bread, it is through no will of ours. No matter a crumb or a loaf. The water we drink comes not from our wishing nor from any endeavor. It is granted. Bestowed. By Him. We must never surrender a drop to our cup, nor crave yet another. For when we lust after something which is not rightfully ours, we have sinned beyond repentance. Yet, we must always endeavor to repent."

She gazed lifelessly into the void before setting her restless eye on Graziella.

"Repentance," the old nun said. "Repentance."

Lowering herself stiffly into the wooden chair at the far end of the table, she motioned for Graziella to sit.

"Let us give thanks."

Leaning forward, she began: "We thank Thee for this meal, O Lord, that which you have bestowed upon us.

For this bread. For this water. Let it fill our bodies as You fill our souls. Let us be thankful for the little we have in this life so that we shall be rewarded in the next. Amen."

Then, mumbling to herself—mumbling words incomprehensible to her keep—the old nun looked coldly at Graziella and said: "Feed yourself. Fill your wretched body with this nourishment. Let it sustain you in the hours that lie ahead."

And extending her bony fingers, she plucked the fly-infested bread and shoved it into her shriveled mouth.

Chapter 9

After the feeding was done—after devouring each crumb on their meager plates, after draining the last driblets of water from the goblets' jagged rims—the old nun arose and drifted out of that gloomy refectory. Graziella followed silently behind, trailing her keeper as she wandered through the abandoned abbey.

After some time, they came upon a breach in the shadows: a vague slither of light barely perceptible. The old nun seized the string of beads dangling by her side and pressed them between her fingers, crushing the head of the broken figure with her bony hand.

"He," she began, setting her eye on Graziella, "has given us two paths."

She pointed to the veil of light hovering before them.

"One leads to salvation," she continued.

She folded the beads deep into her black habit.

"The other," she said, "to eternal damnation."

She muttered beneath her breath—words that Graziella could not comprehend, words that were meant solely for me. Then she descended through the blackness, like a ghost lost to eternity trying to recall the path it had once followed.

At last, she stopped before an ancient gateway that emerged from the shadows—a portal that led to a place that was once dedicated to *him*. Once again, words emerged from her mouth—words only I could comprehend—before dissipating into the musty void.

Having declared her intention—having communicated solely to me—she began removing the heavy barricades that blocked the doorway as Graziella watched like a prisoner, fearful of what lay behind.

"Where do you lead me?" she asked at last, with a tremulous voice that rippled through my heart. "Why do you speak in such riddles? Treat me as if I were a prisoner?"

The old nun continued her labors with no answer until the door swung open and she ushered Graziella into the dark sanctuary.

"Here you shall pray," she said.

She beckoned Graziella to take her place in a cavity of dusty pews that had been furrowed by my anger.

"Pray, Graziella," she commanded. "Pray for redemption. Pray—as if today will be your last."

She gazed upon her keep, mumbled, again, beneath her breath. Then, she turned and exited the chapel, disappearing into the shadows from which she had come.

Graziella peered through the vague shaft of light that trickled down from the crimson-stained windows high above. She eyed the lifeless sanctuary through the faint glow and gazed in horror upon the remains that lay before her —the altar—*his* altar—lying in a heap of dust; the tabernacle, broken in two and lying on its side; the chalice, its shattered remnants scattered among the debris; and, throughout the dark chamber, the statues that had stood tall and solemn, reduced to a pile of rubble. High above, where *his* hideous figure had once reigned, there remained nothing but the faint outline of the cross to which *his* likeness had once been confined. And below, in the shallow pit where she now stood: the empty pews where the nuns and priests had once surrendered themselves in their hopeless quest for salvation.

And then, through the hazy light, she spotted *his* sorry figure, *his* face turned to the wall, *his* implacable expression no longer an edict against my freedom.

It was a masterpiece of malevolence, one which I had rendered in a mighty fit of pique. For when one crosses me after I have delivered, there is no placating my rage. And yet, as I gazed upon the fruits of my fury, I feared the consequences of all I had done, for before me stood what I now saw as the means of my own salvation: an image of beauty and perfection for which I had suddenly fallen and who now quaked at every turn she took.

Graziella held the string of beads the old nun had given her tightly against her chest. Lowering herself into the vacant pew and gazing at the ruins that surrounded her, she made the sign of the cross and cried out in desperation. A wave of fear raced across her delicate face and, at every sudden sound—at each creak that echoed unexpectedly through that moribund chapel—she shuddered. Resigned to her fate, she covered her face with her hands and wept. And then, as desperation gave way to futility, she began, as the old nun had commanded, to pray from the depths of her heart—to pray to *him*, reaching out to *him* for deliverance in a place where I was fully in command.

I squirmed with jealousy. Jealousy churned into anger. Each fervent entreaty that she offered up to *him* made me writhe in rage. Still, my heart melted at each glimpse of her desperation. And then, suddenly, I felt something rise up from deep within me, something I had never before experienced. A feeling that I had observed, over and over, in the men and women who had resisted me throughout the centuries. Was this, I asked, what men throughout the ages had bemoaned? Was this curious feeling what all their foolish verse, what all their maudlin serenades were about? A feeling of yearning? A recognition that, before me stood, at once, perfection and frailty, the human form in all its glory and weakness? A feeling that, try as I might, I could never win the heart of one so innocent, one so pure? One so undetestable!

Suddenly, I was struck with wonder. Suddenly, I yearned to comfort her. I longed to deliver her from the fear that was now conquering her heart. But I knew I could not reveal myself, for I would not be perceived as

I wished. Because, like all men and women, she would shudder at the sight of me and rush to escape, abandon herself once again to the futility of prayer, reach out to *him* for protection only to receive no answer in return.

As if I were more dangerous than the old nun who now held her captive! As if *he* would care more than I!

I remained like this for quite some time: disconsolate, wonderstruck, hidden among the eaves, pondering feelings I had never before felt in my endless, miserable existence, pivoting from indignity to love and back to rage again. Could I, who had been denied all—love, beauty, solace—could I, having been condemned to never-ending damnation, be allowed at last a respite? Could Graziella, in her desperation and need, be a means for my deliverance? My salvation? Even if for just a brief respite? Or would *he*, in all *his* vengeance, continue to torture me? Mock me? Punish me for being nothing more than what *he* had intended? Living out my existence as *he*, *himself*, had meant? Would I be spurned? Struck, as Dryden had once lamented, with a malady that has no cure?

It was I, now, who began to tremble. After an eternity of misery—after squandering my existence spewing havoc in the world, seeking vengeance, tormenting humanity and destroying all their hopes and dreams—I suddenly longed for redemption. Not for any love of *him*. No. *he* deserved nothing but contempt. Nor for some childish notion of piety and forgiveness. No. I, who had struck off in independence, could not stoop to such baseness. I, who had gambled away all for the sake of vanity, for the love of self—for the love of life!—could not now, after all eternity, bow and pray—debase myself—in blind obeisance. No. Graziella was for *me*. For *my* pleasure. For *my* satisfaction. For *my* salvation!

How, I pondered, could I reveal myself? So as not to frighten her—so as not to repulse the one I loved—or, at least, what I perceived, in that moment of weakness, was love, for could love come to one so hideous? So detested? Could one as repulsive as I even be worthy of love? What, after all, did I know of such sentiments? I, whose life had been dedicated solely to hate and evil!

Still, I reasoned, here was a chance for a new start. But how could I make my intentions known? For, as I've already hinted, my form was not the most pleasant. You've read the stories. You've seen the pictures they've conjured of me over the centuries. Oh the iniquity! The unfairness with which I've been treated! And had they been accurate, that would have been the least of my complaints. No, what I looked like was far worse. What I sounded like was something they could never have imagined. My body, dark and scaly—yes, but even more horrid. Malformed. Disproportionate. My wings, once so white and beautiful, now scarred and unwieldy. Scaled and withered. And my face—oh the face that was once so comely! So irresistible! Now utterly repulsive. A face that would evoke nothing but fear. And the voice? The voice! How could a sound once so melodious have become nothing but a harsh groan! Why had *he* rendered me so! Why? After having been the epitome of *his* creation! And you wonder why I detest *him*! You wonder why I seed the world with evil! Create disease and pestilence! Bend benevolence to my wicked will! You wonder why I stay hidden within the shadows. Slithering in corners. Veiled in darkness. So that I can slowly tempt you in your secret pursuits! As I coax you to do things you pretend you could never do! You wonder why one such as I do not reflect in the mirror! Because I refuse to allow it! Because I refuse to look upon myself even as I force those around me to cringe in fear at the very thought of my form!

No, I had to be careful. I had to move ever so quietly. Reveal myself, little by little, so that, once fully exposed, I could be accepted. Pitied, perhaps. Loved—yes loved— like a mother loves even the ugliest of her children. If only once—if just once I could be allowed such love! Just once! Perhaps then I would be able to abandon this life of malevolence forever.

And so I stirred. Ever so softly, so as not to make a sound. Pinned my cumbersome wings as tightly against my wretched body as I could so as not to dislodge a stone or topple the remains of a broken statue. I inched my way forward, slowly, ever so quietly, down through the darkness of that horrid chapel, trying hard not to fall, not to stumble, not to swoop down as I was often wont to do, not to make the least echo of sound. Until suddenly, of no doing of mine, the chandelier—a chandelier once so firm, once so majestic—came tumbling down, and Graziella cried out in terror as it crashed against the remnants of *his* wretched altar.

Her scream was like no other I had heard throughout my baneful existence. I wanted to rush to her. I wanted to hold her; I wanted to comfort her. I wanted to clasp her to my scaly bosom and assure her that she was safe. But I refrained, for I knew her reaction upon seeing me would cause her to swoon. Or, worse: to flee forever. So I stopped myself, remained as still as possible in that moment of pure panic, as she jumped up, inconsolable, and rushed like a mad woman out of that godforsaken chapel.

Chapter 10

I, too, rushed out from that cursed chapel. Rushed with a howl that rumbled through the hollowed hallways and caused the abbey to shake with a violent tremor, that made the mice scurry from their nests and the bats scramble from the crumbling belfries.

As I swooped down from my secret perch, what remained standing came toppling to the ground: the remnants of that detestable altar; the tarnished fragments of the candelabra; the corroded votive stands, their flames long spent, the blue- and red-stained candleholders crashing and shattering. And what relics that lingered burst into powder and scattered throughout that wretched chamber.

Furious, I swooped through the corridors of the abbey, flew with no regard for what stood in my way. Windows burst from their casements. Walls split from the force of my rage. And as I soared through the vacant hallways and chambers, out to the courtyard and down to the catacombs where I knew I would find *my* keep, I left a wake of ruin and destruction. As if all that had been there had not already been destroyed!

Down in those ghastly tombs, past the mummified corpses, in that hellish chamber where Father Francesco had, so long ago, witnessed tortures he had hastened from, cowering under his cowl, I found her: the old nun—Sister Lucretia as you, by now, may have guessed—boiling the oil she had used in her zealous inquisitions, preparing, now, for the fiery bath that had become her constant fate. For that was her destiny, and it was I, not *him*, who had condemned her to her ceaseless tortures. I who had possessed her soul, and I refused to release my fiery grip. Not for anything she had done. Not because she had not complied with my wishes. No. For what she had *not* done for me. For, despite all her wickedness, despite all the ministrations she had performed on my behalf, she had not once recognized my rightful reign, my inescapable supremacy over her soul. Arrogant and insolent, she refused to adore me. Refused, despite her pledges, to fully renounce *him*! As if she could defy my wishes! Usurp my power! And though she had followed my orders—eagerly, unquestionably—she had not bowed to my will. And more— she had dared to challenge me, to rebel against me, as if *she* were the queen of evil, and I her wretched servant. As if *she* were the one to whom all must bow and I a mere wastrel begging at her heels!

As if she could do what she wanted without my consent!

I burst into that grim chamber with a rush of hot wind that singed her desiccated skin. Calmly, she turned toward me with a look of defiance, a look of stoic anticipation, for she understood from the rumblings that reverberated through the caverns that I was in a rage, and she knew the consequences all too well. As if boiling oil were not enough!

As I stood there in the entranceway, my malformed wings trembling with fury, she glared at me with her one good eye—defiant—ready to challenge me yet knowing that she could not prevail.

"What have you done with the girl?" she asked.

She gazed upon me—not with fear, not with awe, but with utter contempt as I stood there in all my hideous glory, bore through her very soul with my fiery eyes, with a look that no other creature could possibly abide. Yet she remained unmoved, stood there glaring at me, adamant, in her stark, black habit.

"I am ready for her," she said, as she quietly stirred the cauldron.

My blood boiled like the oil she was churning, spewed through my charred veins like a burst of lava. Yet I could not answer, for something inside me slowly arose. Something other than hate and evil—a feeling I had not known since I had been cast out of *his* kingdom. A feeling I could not quite define and which left me utterly aghast.

As I watched her prepare her perpetual sentence, my fury slowly settled, and my swollen heart began to shrink. It was a moment of bitter revelation, a moment of calm and clarity—a moment when, normally, my evil machinations would begin to take hold—and yet I realized, after all these centuries, that Sister Lucretia and I had come to an impasse. And worse—that she had become, in her pursuance of evil, my equal.

"The oil is ready," she said. "The chains are prepared."

She pointed to the crypt where she had carried out her most zealous deeds.

"Bring the girl!" she commanded.

She set her glazed eye on my squalid figure, while the other one—the dead one!—began to glow fiercely, as if the fires of hell had suddenly ignited within. Fearless—unfazed by my rage—she stood there, relentless, refusing, as she always had, to recognize my supremacy or to grovel in submission.

"Vile creature!" I shouted, as the force of my rage rose up once again and sent Sister Lucretia flying across the room. "Do you dare to defy me? To behave like a god and ignore my power?"

Sister Lucretia rose from the ground and calmly brushed the dust from her habit.

"I understand," she said. "It can wait. These things can always wait. Eternity is patient with time."

Looking into my wretched eyes, she pointed upward—pointed with the crook of a finger that could no longer be uncurled.

"But there is no escaping what *He* has designed."

Once again, my rage erupted. Once again, I howled in defiance, torched the chamber with my fiery breath and watched as she stood there motionless, her hair, singed, and her skin, charred.

"I could destroy you!" I shouted. "Remove you forever from this world and forbid you the next!"

Imagine, then, her reaction. Imagine how, after years of torment—torment I had inflicted upon her without respite—she had not learned her place. Had not learned a speck of blood's worth of remorse. For she simply looked at me and laughed. Stared coldly upon me with her dreadful eye as if everything I had done to her had been nothing!

"Nonsense," she said. "Only *He* can destroy life. You can only shape it as you will."

We remained like that for some time—she, glowering in her zealousness, and I, knowing that what she had said was true, wishing, like a worm that longs to transform, that I could make it otherwise. I loathed the very words she spat into my face. For I understood, at that very moment, the limits of my powers and, since the tortures I had construed did not seem to faze her, I knew there was nothing more I could do.

"Touch the girl and I will—" I began, but she would not allow me to complete my sentence.

"You will what?"

I could not answer, for there was no torture from which she would turn, no fear that she could not overcome.

"You will what?" she repeated.

She looked upon me with contempt, like a saint ready for martyrdom, like a victor trampling over her vanquished prey.

"Now," she said, beginning to disrobe. "If you will excuse me. I have my ablutions to perform."

And climbing onto the ancient stone tomb which had witnessed her deeds, she jumped into the boiling oil with a shriek that tore through the abbey as I rushed once again through the empty catacombs to mollify my rage.

Chapter 11

While Sister Lucretia was engaged in her penance, Graziella rushed through the abbey like one gripped with a mania that could not be tamed. Need I tell you how she flew from one abandoned room to another, heedless of the darkness that leaped out at each ominous turn? Need I describe how she dodged the vermin scrambling from their burrows? How she evaded the bats that swarmed in a frenzy from the unfettered rafters above? Need I recount each terrified step, each fit of fearfulness that burst within Graziella's soul as she ran through the abbey's twisted bowels following, unwittingly, the very path that Sister Lucretia had warned against?

Need I confess how I suddenly detested the destruction I had created! How I now despised that wicked abbey even more than I despised the one to whom it had been dedicated!

Once again, my heart ached. Once again, I wanted to come to Graziella's rescue, but I recognized the futility of acting upon my as yet unrequited desire. Stunned at my longing to respond to Graziella's predicament, I wrestled with my conscience. Yes, my conscience! For though it was my fate to spread evil wherever possible—to tempt, to persuade, to ensure that only iniquity and perdition infected the world—I was, to my disbelief, seeking to save an innocent creature. To protect her. To deliver her from harm. Yes. From evil. And worse: to gain the love and trust of the one I believed could soothe the eternal burning of my wretched soul. I knew very well it was against my nature. I understood the impossibility of the situation, the utter foolishness of even considering such a notion. My appearance alone would foil my plans. Any attempt to swoop down and whisk her away to safety would only add to her distress. She might die of fright—die and be claimed by *him*, forever beyond my reach. And my design—the one untainted desire I had had in my long, fiendish existence—would be left unattained.

And yet, I continued to believe that there was a way to rescue her—and to save myself!—as I watched her sink further into the quagmire of that accursed cloister. And that I was the only means to her salvation!

Still, I dared not act, for I realized, as Graziella wandered further into that maze of iniquity, that this was yet another manifestation of *his* ruthlessness. It was a lure. A trap. A cruel incarnation of *his* retribution. *his* way of dangling before me a reminder of what I had relinquished so long ago. To torture me for claiming my independence. And through no fault of my own! For it was *he* who had led me to my doom! *his* refusal to forgive! *his* intention, from the very beginning, to create me as *he* had with no possibility of salvation. To make me wallow fully in a life of evil so that *you* could be forewarned against such deeds. And I, to forever bear the blame! For no matter how I might try—no matter what redemptive deeds I might contrive—I would never be able to disentangle myself from the web of wickedness *he* had so cruelly condemned me to.

Once again, *he* stood in my way as I watched Graziella descend further into peril—a cunning reminder that I could never attain even one morsel of happiness.

This realization, which had suddenly revealed itself after an endless passage of time, enraged me such that I almost bellowed out my agony yet again, but I clenched my wretched body as tightly as I could, tightened every monstrous muscle so that not a single sound would emerge. Like a madman who suddenly recognizes his affliction, I was mindful of the consequences of *his* unending retribution, and I knew fully well that, should I make one wrong move, I would at once destroy the unlikely chance I had at happiness. That, once again, *he* would prevail.

And so I watched, wallowing in my wretchedness, as Graziella blindly navigated those endless tunnels, seeking refuge, descending further into the bowels of an abbey that was as unholy as those who had built it. Each passageway led deeper and deeper into the catacombs; each corridor led further into a labyrinth of illusion where escape appeared imminent, a relentless design that reflected the sinister nature of those who had envisioned it. Until, at last, Graziella reached the far side of the burial grounds where the horrors of that ghastly dungeon awaited her.

I had to act quickly. To find a way to prevent Graziella from continuing down that path where she would end up as another victim in Sister Lucretia's unrelenting quest for redemption.

It was then that the answer came to me, materialized, at once, in my nefarious mind, like a spirit emerging from eternal sleep. Arising like a cadaver from its restless grave, the solution revealed itself as palpably as the calcified corpses which now gazed upon Graziella from their icy orb of sleep. For as Graziella abruptly ceased her running, she gazed in horror upon the desiccated remains of untended cadavers scattered throughout that burial chamber—unentombed corpses that had mummified over time, petrified into ghastly postures, their opaque eyes wide with terror, their brittle skin crumbling, their ashen skeletons exposed. And out of that macabre mixture of parched skin and mottled bone, a simple solution revealed itself, one as swift and plain as death itself.

And so, at that very moment, as Graziella stared in terror at the chilling scene she had stumbled upon, Father Francesco arose from that field of death, awakened by me from his eternal sleep, just as he had awakened that fateful morning, so long ago, from his bed, as alive with anxiety as he had been when Sister Lucretia and her unwilling minions were busy with their sinister deeds. Fresh from his deathly spell of sleep, Father Francesco appeared, as if he had just left that horrid chamber, with a look of terror on his face and a pall of irreconcilable regret hanging over his revivified soul.

I watched, with a wicked sense of pleasure and triumph, as he, once again, surrendered to his cowardly conscience and ran until he was faced suddenly with a spectacle he had not seen in all his years, one that contradicted fully the horrors he had left behind, so long ago, and the rigid vows that had been imposed on that monastery's residents. For there before him stood Graziella, like an angel, her beauty barely visible through her robe and hood, trembling from head to foot—flesh and blood, alive and breathing, unlike the lifeless bodies scattered about.

Father Francesco ceased his rapid advance and stared incredulously at Graziella as if hypnotized, as every bone and muscle in his newly resuscitated body took on a new life—a life he had not known since entering the grave—a life he had not imagined even when he had been alive. Graziella stared at him, frightened, unsure if this was yet another phantom, secreted in this horrid place. Yet, comforted by his comely face and his priestly garb, she reached out her hand. Then, without warning, she turned and ran as Sister Lucretia's strident shrieks suddenly echoed through the dank caverns.

"Stop!" he shouted.

It was half command, half plea, but Graziella did not

heed, and Father Francesco took off after her as she fled past the petrified corpses, past toppled tombs and gaping crypts until, faced with a shadow that slinked up ahead, she stopped and fell to her knees, surrendering to the inevitable and sobbing like a child whose nightmare refuses to dissipate even upon awakening.

Father Francesco knelt down beside her and gently placed his hand on her head, lifting her face so he could see her.

"You are safe here," he said.

But looking around and seeing nothing except death and destruction, Graziella was unable to stop her crying, to calm her nerves, to take comfort in a man whose demeanor belied the gruesome atmosphere that surrounded them.

"What is your name?" he asked.

"Graziella."

Her tender lips trembled, her tears fell uncontrollably, and her bosom rose and fell to the rhythm of the fearsome storm that was raging inside her fragile soul. How I wanted to comfort her! How I wanted, yet again, to reveal myself, fold her under my blackened wings and blind her to those vicious horrors!

"Why do you roam these unwelcome chambers?" Father Francesco asked.

As she was about to answer, her eyes opened wide in terror.

Father Francesco rose and turned as Sister Lucretia approached, a scourge in one hand, a chain in the other.

"Good," she said calmly. "You have brought the girl. It

is time for her to repent."

He took a step forward, now filled with strength, and I knew, as I watched him look straight into Sister Lucretia's wicked eye, that, this time, he would not shirk his duty, for he had been captivated by Graziella and would not allow her to be harmed. Still, I whispered quietly into his ear, whispered so he would know exactly what to say, infused him with a sense of courage he had never before known.

"You cannot have her," he said.

His voice was loud and strong, and his demeanor was such that one might cower at the very sight of him.

Sister Lucretia sneered at his attempt at valor, for she knew well his timidity, knew well that, despite the authority he had been endowed with, so long ago, he had never been able to exercise even one ounce of power.

"Would you stand between me and Him?" she said. "Would you defy His will?"

"In the name of God, Sister Lucretia," he insisted. "I will not let you touch this innocent creature."

"Innocent?" Sister Lucretia said. "What do you know about innocence, Father Francesco? You run, as always. You run from me as if I were the devil himself. You run from the sacred responsibilities that He has granted you. But I have repented my deeds. I have repented as you have not. And I *will* carry out the will of God."

"The will of God! Is God so vengeful that he demands such cruelty? Is God so ruthless that even the innocent must suffer? Is that what you call the will of God? Is there no contrition? No possibility of forgiveness? No opportunity to ask for His blessing and seek His absolution?"

"And what have you done, Father Francesco, to earn absolution? What have you done to purge your sins? I know your sins, Father Francesco. Intimately."

"I have prayed, Sister Lucretia. I have prayed, night and day. And my conscience is as clear as the sky that looks down upon us at dawn."

"Give me the girl," she insisted. "She must repent. We must all repent."

"I will not," Father Francesco replied.

"Do you defy me then? Do you defy His will?"

And then there arose a silence—a silence broken only by Graziella's quiet whimpering and the unspoken sorrow of the corpses whose eternal pain seemed louder than the endless shrieks of hell. And my heart stopped as I waited for Father Francesco to act, as I waited for him to repeat the words I had commanded him to say, and, when I could no longer bear it, I whispered once again into his ear.

"I am the abbot here," he said. "Go now. Go and cleanse your soul. Cleanse the thoughts that fill your wicked heart. Cleanse them and leave us in peace."

And then Father Francesco took Graziella's hand and lifted her to her feet and led her out of that bleak chamber, led her up, through the twisted catacombs and toward the light of day as Sister Lucretia looked upon them in stony silence.

Chapter 12

Nor did Father Francesco fail to be taken by Graziella's unyielding charm, for, as he led her through the musty catacombs and up the stone steps that led up to that haunted abbey, he noticed, with a rekindled eye, her enigmatic form, hidden, as it were, beneath the cloak she had wound snugly around her body.

A strange feeling raced through his newly awakened loins, a sensation he had not experienced since long before his entry into the grave, one I had instilled in him in his youth and which he now attempted to suppress as he had done so many times during his cloistered existence. Even the cold kiss of death, which had rendered him unfeeling for eternity, could not temper the flare of desire that now erupted within. As he proceeded up the forbidden steps, he observed Graziella's slender body from the corner of his eye and grappled with the rosary tangled deep within his ragged cowl, seeking deliverance from the hopeless prayers he mumbled in haste.

Graziella—the woman who had smitten me like no other throughout eternity, the woman who had become the sole object of my existence—followed Father Francesco, and wondered where he was leading her, wondered if this priest—this being who had appeared out of nowhere—was someone who could be trusted. Wondered, as the lifeless soul I had reincarnated guided her through the maze of death and destruction, his gaze falling fitfully upon her—wondered if he, like Sister Lucretia, was something other than what he appeared to be.

A sudden chill embraced Graziella. Drawing the strings of her cloak ever more tightly around her tender neck, she watched Father Francesco climb the narrow steps that led from this hopeless scene of death back to the ghostly corridors of the abbey. To comfort her, I whispered into her ears. Whispered words of assurance to assuage the pall of fear that had settled on her soul.

Graziella repeated the words I recited, repeated them as if they were hers—*A holy man. A man dedicated to the church*—as she followed the lifeless abbot through the devastation that embraced every corner of the abbey. Yet, though the words echoed within her mind, she failed to believe, failed to abandon what her eyes clearly told her. For there was a strange aura about him. An air that belied his appearance. His eyes were blank. His lips were pale and lifeless. His words were devoid of feeling. And his body seemed listless, as if he had just arisen from a long, feverish illness. As if the trappings of the priesthood—the cowl from which his ashen hands emerged—were meant to cover up something not quite holy, something more sinister.

"Father," she said at last. "Where are you taking me?"

And then, before he had a chance to answer: "Father, I'm frightened."

Father Francesco wrestled with the beads knotted around his lifeless fingers. Having traversed the fallen corridors, he stopped beside the dreary cell where Sister Lucretia had fist led Graziella and paused. Making the sign of the cross, he looked at Graziella and said: "You must rest, my child. You are weary."

He gazed upon her, gazed with longing, gazed with a fear of retribution, knowing that it was incumbent upon him to protect the innocent from evil and to protect his soul from damnation.

"Rest now. I will be nearby."

He turned in haste, clutching his beads, hesitated, then rushed off into the murky darkness.

But if Father Francesco thought he could get away so easily—if he believed that temptation could be brushed aside and forgotten—he was mistaken. For I had other plans. For him and for Graziella. For unlike Father Francesco, I would not resist temptation; I had no qualms about getting what I wanted. And if I myself could not satiate my desire, he would be the instrument through which it would be attained. Just as it had been in the past. It was simply a matter of convincing, of allowing him to recognize the goodness in the evil he perceived. It would take time. But time, after all, is something I have no shortage of. And the weakness of men knows no bounds.

And so I watched as Graziella, weary and fearful, settled herself into her dreary cell. Outside, an oppressive darkness set in, and the doleful sound of an owl pierced the heavy silence. The shadows of day slowly dissipated and merged into the relentless blackness of night, bathed in the glow of a moon which bled through the splintered window and caused the creatures of darkness to rise and take life.

Graziella was soon overcome by drowsiness—a heavy stupor I had conjured—and she approached the narrow bed and disrobed, revealing, through the meager vestments that still adorned her, the full extent of her exquisite form. Unable to stay awake—unable to resist the siren song of sleep—she cradled her head between her slender arms and fell into a restless slumber.

It was a magnificent sight, and I gazed upon her from the shadows, as she lay in full repose, her rapid breathing inflating her gentle breast.

When I was certain she had fully succumbed to the blindfolds of sleep, I approached, softly, quietly, so as not to wake her, and stood beside that wretched bed, yearning to quench my desires. My fiery eyes ignited the darkness and my hot breath filled the room with the intensity of a summer squall. Such was my passion that I had merely to blink to set that room and everything in it ablaze.

I could have had her right then and there, could have possessed her fully, carried her off into my realm of darkness to reside with me for all eternity. My queen. My partner now and forever. That was the least I deserved to quell this long, lonesome existence: someone to share my everlasting misery. For *he* had created man and woman for each other's comfort, while I had been abandoned, exiled, left alone and forlorn. Was I to remain this way till the end of time? How could I continue to bear this torture? No, this was the least I could have: this precious creature, this embodiment of human perfection. It was the least *I* could claim from the whole of *his* wretched creation after he had, in utter arrogance, cast me off into perdition.

Here she lay, ready for my burning embrace. But suddenly she stirred. Suddenly, she thrashed about, flailing her slender arms in an unconscious panic. Perhaps she had heard me. Perhaps she had sensed my unwelcome presence. Or perhaps she was in the midst of a nightmare—an apparition as monstrous as mine, one that had seized her in her sleep, as I loomed commandingly above her.

And then I heard what she herself had heard, in her somnolent state, and, at once, I understood. It was the sound of something melancholy, something not quite real—a mournful melody which arose faintly in the distance and summoned her from the realms of slumber.

Graziella opened her eyes and rose from her bed, mesmerized by the odd music that beckoned her from beyond those ancient walls, and I was forced, once again, to obscure myself in the darkness. Forced, once again, to merely look upon her as she made her way toward the window and the sounds that beckoned from beyond. Forced, once again, to hide in the shadows and postpone the consummation of my aching desire.

Outside, the moon burned, and Graziella, caught between wakefulness and sleep, was drawn forward by its enticing rays. Peering through the splintered panes of glass, she watched as the courtyard burst into life with the ghosts of those who had suffered the torments of the abbey. A strident revelry of shrieks and howls filled every corner of that cursed dwelling. It was a glum gathering, an assembly of tormented souls, a congregation of those who, like Graziella, had found their way here, who had ended their days in ways contrary to human nature, and who now spent eternity lost in an everlasting purgatory, wandering the ethers and seeking what respite they could find.

The music played and the singers moaned as, one by one, the wretched revelers appeared, for it was a call to those who had come under the abbey's spell, an invitation to those who had not survived its twisted deeds, a summons to rise up from the dead and seek the elusive comfort of Lethe.

There they assembled, in that melancholy courtyard, the tortured and the murdered, those who had been chained and starved, those whose flesh had been peeled, whose bodies had been boiled in oil, whose eyes had been dashed out, those who had been imprisoned and left to waste away: all mere skeletons of their dismal past, celebrating the parting from a life of torment into the freedom of eternity. Out of their cold graves they arose, up from the dreary catacombs, out into that squalid court for a night of revelry—shadows of men and women, young and old, and those who had not quite made it into life—and here they gathered, here they danced a macabre minuet, here they reveled in death's cadaverous ball, danced to the dark rhythms of death's relentless baton.

How can I describe more fully what Graziella beheld? How can I relay to you what horrors she witnessed in the twilight of sleep, of those who, like her, innocent and unaware, had ended up here in this abbey, seeking sanctuary, seeking solace, seeking escape from whatever sorrows had befallen them, ignorant of what awaited within: men and women of the cloth, garbed in the veils of piety, bent, in their pious ignorance, on enforcing their uncompromising interpretation of *his* stringent will.

And I, of course, had been behind it all. For I had taken his commandments and wrought them into a mockery of all *he* had proudly bestowed upon the world. And in doing so, I had forced Sister Lucretia and her underlings into their ghoulish deeds. I had made sure that this edifice, built out of blind reverence, would sink into the lowest ideals that man could possibly reach. And I had succeeded! I, through my powers—the powers *he* had neglected to take from me—had corrupted every man and woman who stepped through that abbey's rusted gates, had made sure that each of them would suffer as *he* had made me suffer.

All except Father Francesco, who had resisted me with his prayers and cowardice. And Sister Lucretia, who had obeyed me until the very end, until, suddenly realizing what she had willingly done, and having sought, when it was too late, repentance from *him*, abandoned me and my favors and attempted to purge the sins she had eagerly committed. But even then, she could not resist my influence! Even now she crumbles under the strength of my will.

And now, these poor lifeless creatures, who had suffered under the hands of my followers, who had wished for death to escape the agonies imposed upon them, emerged from the dark chambers of eternity to remember, to haunt, to infest the place that had deceived them. And there was nothing I could do to stop them, for this was their respite from eternal damnation, their chance, granted by *him*, to escape, temporarily, from the judgment of torture.

Graziella looked on through eyes veiled in sleep, the muscles on her face rippling, the skin around her delicate mouth twitching from the horror she now witnessed. Soon, I feared, she might fully awake. Soon, she might fully comprehend the secrets of this dark, heartless abbey.

Round and round they went, in a wicked waltz led by death's unsparing baton, as the tempo increased and the music crescendoed until the courtyard was soon a frenzy of charred bone and rotten flesh, filled with the wails of creation's most wretched souls.

Until they turned. Until they began to approach the window where I stood, behind Graziella, watching and waiting for this hopeless gala to come to an end. The earth shook with their immortal anger. The abbey, already in disarray, creaked and trembled. What was loose became dislodged. What was standing toppled over. Stones flew and walls crumbled as that horde of unsolaced souls sensed my presence and focused their unrequited anger on me.

I feared for Graziella. I feared that the one prize in all eternity that I truly cherished—the one I would claim despite whatever efforts *he* would employ—would perish in this maelstrom of rage. So I lifted her, gently so she would not fully awake, would not consciously witness the horrors that surrounded her, carried her to her bed, shielded her with my huge black wings and waited for the sun to rise and disperse those vengeful creatures who, thanks to me, would never know even one moment of rest.

Chapter 13

Graziella awoke at dawn—awoke with a shriek that echoed through the shrill corridors of that haunted abbey. Her voice rang with terror and shattered the morning silence, wending its way through my wretched heart and arousing a twinge of pity. And her eyes—those eyes!—swollen with fear, as she leaped from the bed and wrapped her cloak around her trembling body! Her face was tinged with panic as she rushed toward the window where the last shadows of the night slinked away! It tore at my soul, made me quiver with anguish—and yes, with a prickly sense of pleasure—as I remained hidden within the last burning embers of the fireplace and grappled with a passion that made my eyes smolder.

Graziella peered through the shattered glass. A dull recollection arose and tugged against her consciousness with its elusive arms, as she gazed, bewildered, at the empty courtyard and held herself tight against the morning chill.

My spirit—damned as it was, stoked in the flames of iniquity—burned with a sense of pleasure as I witnessed the waves of terror consume her soul. From the dying ashes of that ancient hearth, I gazed upon her with a feeling I could not define—a feeling of sadness which captivated me and a poignant flame of desire that pulsed like the ebbing cinders in which I lay. My heart throbbed with a strange sense of sorrow as I watched her surrender to the terror that arose within and seized her with its relentless claws.

Soon, the grim silence was broken as the sound of rushing feet reverberated through the empty hallway and the nervous clanging of keys shattered the morning quiet. The door opened and Father Francesco appeared, as anxious as I was allured. Like a madman, he rushed inside as if he had lost his final senses.

Gazing wildly around the dim chamber, his pale face cloaked in apprehension, he spotted the toppled chest, the splintered window through which the cold remnants of drizzle trickled, the cracks that slithered down the brittle walls as if they were alive. Then his eyes fell upon *his* book—that foul volume lying over-turned on the ground—and he hastily conjured the sign of the cross and rushed across the room to salvage it.

"It was merely a tremor," he said.

He kissed the accursed volume and held it against his chest.

"A small tremor," he said. "A sign of God's displeasure."

"No!" she shouted.

Graziella shook her head. She wanted to believe him, but she trembled as she recalled what she had seen, the horrors that seemed as tangible now as Father Francesco did, standing before her, ghostly like the phantoms who had haunted her turbulent sleep.

She tried to convince herself that it had just been a bad dream. A nightmare that had emerged from within, one that had manifested itself from all that had occurred since her arrival. But she was unable to forget the image of all those tortured souls who had gathered in the midst of night, unable, now, under the warm rays of the rising sun, to shake off the memory. Instead, in this dark room where the fireplace throbbed without a spark of warmth, in this frigid abbey where she had sought refuge and had found menace instead, in this room where she trembled from the cold as she looked upon the destruction outside and the devastation within—as she gazed upon Father Francesco as if he had just emerged from that horde of haunted revelers—she could not dispel the macabre apparitions from her mind, for they seemed as real as the gaunt figure of Farther Francesco who stood before her, a palpable specter in this enigmatic abbey.

"They are common here," Father Francesco continued, as if she needed further convincing.

But even he did not believe these words. Even he knew the realities of this forbidden place, for he had witnessed them throughout his long tenure. Had run from them. Had taken his very own life to finally escape!

"No!" she shouted again, trembling. "There is something evil here. I can feel it."

He lowered his eyes in shame, struggled to suppress the deception that had overtaken him, and folded the book shut. Then, he kissed it once again—kissed it while his eyes gazed upon Graziella—and gently set it on top of the mantel.

"One must always protect His book," he said quietly.

Graziella stared in silence. The chill of the morning caused her to shiver as her mind wrestled with the shadows of the night that would not retreat from her memory.

"They are here," she said. "I saw them—out there."

"There's no one here. Just you and me."

"The dead," she cried. "They're alive."

"The dead are gone, Graziella. Gone to their graves. Gone to entreat His mercy."

"I can feel them. In these walls. In every corner of this horrid place."

"It was just a dream. An unholy dream that seized you in a restless sleep."

"No. They were out there. Moaning and wailing. Dancing, as if they were alive. And you. Who are you? Why do you live in this horrid place? Surrounded by death?"

"God does not allow such hauntings in His holy places. God forgives and allows for eternal rest."

Graziella shook her head in disbelief, as if she understood that the words emerging from his mouth did not belong to him. And they did not, for it was I who provided them, I who fed him every utterance, every phrase, every sentence. And Graziella listened in disbelief. Listened to him—to me!—as the remnants of the night faded into day, as the morning, rising with a semblance of life, began to fill the air and imbue that lifeless room.

"Come now," Father Francesco said, extending his hand. "We must go and pray. We must ask Him to dispel the evil that has suddenly set its wretched hands upon you."

Slowly, he approached her, as his eyes widened and an unholy rapture overcame him, until he grazed her finger with his icy touch.

Graziella jumped back. She looked around, searching for escape, and just as I was about to whisper words of comfort into her ear, to mesmerize her so that she would succumb, she turned and ran straight into the arms of Sister Lucretia who, at that very moment, appeared in the doorway. Graziella fell to her knees, surrendering to the waves of terror that overcame her and the fate that she knew must be hers.

"I heard the disturbance, Father Francesco," Sister Lucretia said.

"It was just a nightmare," Father Francesco answered.

He looked up at Sister Lucretia, his eyes ablaze.

"They are common in one so young," she responded. "I will take her to my room."

"I will leave her in your good hands."

Calmly, as if the evil I had instilled in him suddenly dissipated, he looked upon Graziella like one tending his flock and blessed her with the sign of the cross. Then, he exited the room and faded into the darkness.

"Come, Graziella," Sister Lucretia said, lifting her up. "We must purge the evil that has conquered your soul."

Chapter 14

How do you describe evil cloaked in the stiff, white wimple of piety? Such iniquity, such deception, such cruelty in the guise of reverence knows no equivalent in words or humankind. Nor does such treachery. For of all Sister Lucretia's imperfections, this last was her hallmark and, by far, the worst!

Of course, she was a product of my handiwork. A protégé. A disciple who, torn between her lust for devotion—torn between *him* and me—eventually spurned me—donned her black habit once again and secured it so tightly, even I could not slip in between its pleated folds. Yet, she was a marvel to behold—a work shaped by my ardent hands. Even now, as she emerges, each time, from her scalding ablutions, she struggles as if still possessed.

Once an untouched soul, as she entered that order of nuns whose sole purpose was dedication to abstention and solitude, she soon succumbed to my hidden charms, my soft whispers, my subtle, unsavory suggestions, my inescapable temptations, my irresistible enticements, and she became part of my world. A part of me! Anyone at that tender age, embarking on an illusive mission of humility and chastity, would have found it difficult to resist my allure. Anyone, that is, who did not have the strength and wisdom to resist seduction, to fortify resolve, in order to adhere to that stringent way that is the life of the cloistered.

When I first stumbled upon her—or, rather, she upon me—she was just a novice in that order of nuns that had taken root in what was then known as the Abbey of San Pietro. As a child, she dreamed of dedicating her life to *him* and, when she came of age and her parents dutifully presented her with suitors to convince her to ignore the hallowed call and succumb instead to the ways of the world, she refused each one, spurned the comely and the rich, the humble and the heartfelt, and proclaimed that she had been chosen to commune only with the one she considered supreme to all.

Naturally, I could not abide this, for my jealousy knows no bounds. I yearned to woo her away, make her succumb to my brazen wishes. And so when her parents failed to convince her that a cloistered life was one that required stamina and, above all, will, I intervened, naturally on their behalf, tried my best to convince her to abandon her dreams and join in the pleasures of the flesh. For that, after all, is the essence of man and woman. That, after all, is the justification for marriage: to sanctify what is otherwise considered unholy.

But like her parents, I failed. And while they finally gave in, rejoiced even, at the final decision, as they made their long, arduous journey to the abbey to deliver her into the hands of the Mother Superior, I swore to all that was unsanctified that I would persist. That I would win. For once again, *he* had deprived me of my rightful command.

Soon, she learned the ways of the veil and settled into a life of simplicity and sacrifice. Each morning, she would rise at dawn with hope in her heart. Each evening, as doubt wormed its way between her and her sacred rosary, it gnawed at her very soul and reminded her of all she had abandoned. Gradually, I intercepted her every thought, infiltrated each prayer, each delicate supplication for forgiveness. Like any angel worth his wings, I whispered, ever so gently, into her ears. And true to my unangelic nature, I filled her mind with visions that no novice, no child of that innocent age, should ever contemplate—distracted her mind from prayer, caused her smooth, unblemished flesh to quiver with feelings she had never before known, feelings she would ever want to satisfy. Night and day, I saturated her mind until, as time went on, she could no longer bear it.

Soon, her pious prayers were replaced with unspeakable sensations—sensations from which there was no escape, feelings that became no nun, let alone a novitiate whose dedication to *him* soon came into question. And gradually, after carefully luring her, after caressing her soul and kindling her flesh, she became a different kind of novice—one that would change the face of that ill-fated monastery forever.

For, as you already know, the abbey also housed that order of monks to which Father Francesco belonged. Father Francesco. The good-natured monk. That humble, pious, pure individual for whom that wretched book—those words and fables that forever defined me in the most heinous of terms—meant more than anything else in this world. Each day, he approached it like an eager lover, each day, dutifully bathed before he touched it, made his ablutions, purified himself, covered himself in the cleanest of cowls. And then, only then, would he approach it, lift it gently in his hands, kiss it tenderly, lovingly part its pages, pour himself into it as if he were pouring himself for the first time into a virgin lover. And then, ecstatic, satiated to the fullest, his face flush with the aura of one who has just slaked his senses, he would kiss it, once again, adoringly, lay it gently beside his bed and fall into the deepest, most satisfying of slumbers before waking for yet another ardent tryst.

I knew, when I first set my glaring eyes on him from behind those secluded walls, as I watched him sleeping peacefully in his humble bed, that he was my chosen one, that he would be the means for fully possessing Sister Lucretia. And, in the end, the means to possessing all the sorry souls who inhabited that cursed monastery. Because anyone—anything dedicated solely to *him*—any individual who refused to acknowledge my wishes and succumb to my pleasures, was doomed to a destiny of misery. For doubt is the worst of all tortures for those who would otherwise believe.

So early one morning, during matins, when the holy monks and nuns were gathered in the candlelit chapel for the completion of their nocturnal prayers, and the solemn psalms were at last coming to a close, that ill-starred assembly of nuns and monks arose and filed silently from their weary pews, each genuflecting, one by one, before *his* pitiful image as they parted to their meager cells for a bit of welcome respite. The smell of incense, the acrid odor of burning wax, filled the hushed chamber, and drowsiness, mixed with an element of elusive elation, imbued the bodies and souls of those fatigued congregants with an intangible sense of satisfaction as they descended from their ethereal heights and slowly settled back into the world of the mundane.

Sister Lucretia, as yet unaccustomed to long nights of nocturnes and vigils, slid sleepily from her creaking pew, treaded, languidly, to the front of the chapel, genuflected gracefully before *his* sad figure and then, as she rose from her knees, suddenly tumbled to the ground. It was a short-lived faint, a brief spell of fatigue which quickly, and with no warning, overcame her worn body and penetrated her weary soul. Father Francesco, standing just behind her in the narrow aisle, rushed to her side and gently lifted her—lifted her, upon my coaxing—and looked, with a feeling he had never before known, into her eyes, as her face flushed instantly with a trace of shame.

Perhaps it was the time of morning that caused such weakness to overcome or the fact that they had both kept the long night in deep contemplation, something which wore on body and soul, but the sensation Sister Lucretia experienced, as Father Francesco raised her up from the ground, had more to do with his sudden touch than with the embarrassment of falling before the entire congregation. The warm glow on his striking face, the ardor in his deep brown eyes as he gazed innocently into her own, evoked feelings hitherto suppressed by prayer and deprivation.

Immediately, I took advantage of the situation as you would imagine I might, for at that very moment, a spark flashed through both of their bodies—a spark not quite discernible but one that ignited feelings neither had ever contemplated, for when one joins the monastery, such thoughts, such desires, are forever abandoned, left behind, sealed away as firmly as the monastery door, as it shuts with a formidable echo, cutting off the initiate from any thought of worldly communion.

Thoughts, forgotten—forbidden—until I come along. Until I see fit.

Father Francesco, sensing an impropriety, lowered his glance, as a hint of the illicit brushed against his consciousness. He mumbled a desperate supplication and, without a word, turned and rushed to the safety of his cell.

But passions are not so easily tempered. Desire and gratification are not so simply dispensed with. Once ignited, the flame is hard to snuff. Once recognized, it cannot so easily be pushed aside, for it will gnaw at the very core, implant itself in both body and mind, intrude on every waking thought and manifest itself insidiously in sleep—and, yes, even in prayer.

So it was with Father Francesco. And so it was with Sister Lucretia who was about to be initiated into a life she had never before contemplated.

As the days went by and they passed each other in dutiful silence—in the hallways or the courtyard or, even, dare I say, in the chapel—their minds became distracted from prayer as their eyes fell inadvertently upon each other.

Gradually, things took an inevitable turn. At first a subtle smile. Then, a tentative glance. Finally, a brazen nod. And soon these would lead down a path to which there is no possibility of escape.

It happened, one morning, behind the sacristy where Father Francesco had gone to cleanse the chalice and polish the paten, both just used in the morning's service. Sister Lucretia, deep in contemplation, lost in prayer, wandered in—by mistake, perhaps, or by some stroke of fate which she could not escape. Or by my directive—a directive to which she was not aware. Faced with happenstance, they smiled briefly, nodded apologetically in recognition that this unintended encounter was forbidden. And then, as they struggled to extricate themselves from this compromising stroke of fate, they brushed lightly against each other as they rushed away, each to their own cell.

Gradually, these accidental meetings increased—unintentionally, or so it seemed—for soon they occurred less by chance and more by whim, each time leading to a liberty that became more brazen than the previous.

Oh the power of desire! How inescapable it is! How easily it guides! How surreptitious its hands! How remarkable the ease with which it concludes!

And so it was, early one morning, after the long night's vigil had come to an end, as the good monks and nuns made their way, separately and silently, to their individual cells. Father Francesco suddenly changed course, for reasons unfathomable to him, made his way quickly down the dark hallway that led to the catacombs. And Sister Lucretia, glancing from beneath her nervous veil and sensing something she could not comprehend, followed, down into the darkness, through the deep corridors where the dead were as yet resting peacefully, down to a secret chamber where Father Francesco nervously awaited her. It was a chamber where he had often toiled, chiseling tombs and sculpting saints, but where, now, something else would be rendered by those delicate hands.

Sister Lucretia's heart was pounding furiously. Her body was trembling, her flesh tingling with a sensation she alone could not appease.

Not a word was spoken in that chamber as they faced each other. Not a prayer was uttered, not an excuse, not even an attempt at a feigned apology, for when two adults contemplate an act and find themselves at each other's disposal, not one word need be said.

I need not tell you what went on in that tender chamber. I need not describe the rustling of clothes, the sighs of pleasure, the cries of delight that echoed through the lifeless catacombs as they came together and fulfilled their purpose. There is nothing new here, nothing to describe that has not before been described, no feeling to illuminate which has not already been exalted.

And so I will leave you to your imagination. I will leave you, for a moment, in that dark room, as you muse over each kiss, contemplate each embrace, imagine each touch and envision what took place that fatal morning, below, in the catacombs of that fated abbey, beneath cowl and veil, in the bowels of a sacred church whose hallowed grounds were now to become irreversibly defiled.

Chapter 15

But we have forgotten Graziella. Ushered through the dark corridors by Sister Lucretia. Haunted by ghostly apparitions. Having cried out in terror from a chamber where even the most devout could not hope for deliverance. Having been comforted by Father Francesco, a monk whose motives were as uncertain as his tenuous existence. Graziella, now in the care of one whose existence had been forged by my fiery hands. Graziella, the one I longed to swathe under my once angelic wings. The one I hungered for, yearned to anoint as my eternal queen. *My* Graziella. Now in the grasp of a creature who had turned her back on me. An ungodly nun who, having once succumbed to my will, now refused to abide by even the simplest murmur from my foul lips. Lucretia: whose cinched shadow preceded her as she wound her way in silence through the narrow corridors. Whose stiff black habit cut through the silence as it scratched against the abbey's walls. Whose gaunt face, illuminated by the meager light that penetrated the narrow corridors through which she led her prisoner, floated through the shadows as if severed from its shrouded trunk.

Silently, they trod: Graziella and Lucretia. Silently—though an occasional whimper escaped from my love's trembling lips. Though her breathing throbbed as she tried to ascertain if the figure, walking mutely beside her, was alive or if, instead, it belonged to that unearthly gathering of revelers she had witnessed outside her window.

At last, they stopped, and Graziella gasped as Lucretia unlocked the door to her cell, a small, sparsely furnished chamber not unlike the one in which Graziella herself had been imprisoned. But where the fire in hers had settled into a lifeless pile of embers, Lucretia's blazed with a fiery wrath. In the corner, a hastily repaired table cradled her breviary, its torn pages carefully mended with a thin black thread. In the center stood a small, wooden bed—an unwelcoming resting place covered by a flimsy white cloth. And nailed to the wall above—a cross. Once a crucifix that embraced *him*, now a mere frame from which *his* semblance had been ripped. Left behind: the rotten wood on which *he* had been draped and the rusted nails which had fastened *him* to his fate.

"Rest, Graziella," Sister Lucretia said, shattering the stillness. "Rest your wicked body. For your penance will soon begin."

She stared into the fireplace and mumbled into the flames—strange utterances that echoed back into the room as her face reddened and her dead eye brimmed with the fire's reflection. Gradually, her voice mutated into a hollow groan, until, without moving her lips, she spoke in a tone that no longer resembled her own.

the building shook. Again, the floors rattled. Again, the walls quaked. Again, Graziella—my sweet, sweet Graziella—the one who had unknowingly captured my heart—watched in horror as the world around her swiftly disintegrated.

the building shook. Again, the floors rattled. Again, the walls quaked. Again, Graziella—my sweet, sweet Graziella—the one who had unknowingly captured my heart—watched in horror as the world around her swiftly disintegrated.

Chapter 15

But we have forgotten Graziella. Ushered through the dark corridors by Sister Lucretia. Haunted by ghostly apparitions. Having cried out in terror from a chamber where even the most devout could not hope for deliverance. Having been comforted by Father Francesco, a monk whose motives were as uncertain as his tenuous existence. Graziella, now in the care of one whose existence had been forged by my fiery hands. Graziella, the one I longed to swathe under my once angelic wings. The one I hungered for, yearned to anoint as my eternal queen. *My* Graziella. Now in the grasp of a creature who had turned her back on me. An ungodly nun who, having once succumbed to my will, now refused to abide by even the simplest murmur from my foul lips. Lucretia: whose cinched shadow preceded her as she wound her way in silence through the narrow corridors. Whose stiff black habit cut through the silence as it scratched against the abbey's walls. Whose gaunt face, illuminated by the meager light that penetrated the narrow corridors through which she led her prisoner, floated through the shadows as if severed from its shrouded trunk.

Silently, they trod: Graziella and Lucretia. Silently—though an occasional whimper escaped from my love's trembling lips. Though her breathing throbbed as she tried to ascertain if the figure, walking mutely beside her, was alive or if, instead, it belonged to that unearthly gathering of revelers she had witnessed outside her window.

At last, they stopped, and Graziella gasped as Lucretia unlocked the door to her cell, a small, sparsely furnished chamber not unlike the one in which Graziella herself had been imprisoned. But where the fire in hers had settled into a lifeless pile of embers, Lucretia's blazed with a fiery wrath. In the corner, a hastily repaired table cradled her breviary, its torn pages carefully mended with a thin black thread. In the center stood a small, wooden bed—an unwelcoming resting place covered by a flimsy white cloth. And nailed to the wall above—a cross. Once a crucifix that embraced *him*, now a mere frame from which *his* semblance had been ripped. Left behind: the rotten wood on which *he* had been draped and the rusted nails which had fastened *him* to his fate.

"Rest, Graziella," Sister Lucretia said, shattering the stillness. "Rest your wicked body. For your penance will soon begin."

She stared into the fireplace and mumbled into the flames—strange utterances that echoed back into the room as her face reddened and her dead eye brimmed with the fire's reflection. Gradually, her voice mutated into a hollow groan, until, without moving her lips, she spoke in a tone that no longer resembled her own.

"I can feel it, Graziella. I can feel the wickedness within you. I can sense the sin that blackens your soul. The evil thoughts. The filthy desires! You cannot hide them."

And then, pinning Graziella with her fiery eye, she said: "We must cleanse your soul. We must purge you of all you have done until you become as pure as the fire."

The flames swelled, and Lucretia's voice faded away. Slowly, the fire spread until it licked her habit with its fiery tongue. Then, the flames engulfed her, and she turned once again to her ward and gazed upon her with a look that burned through my Graziella's tender flesh.

Graziella winced and screamed as Lucretia extended her fiery hands like a witch whose heart was as black as the habit that nourished the tongues of fire.

"Fall to your knees, Graziella," Lucretia shrieked. "Confess all you have done. Pray for His mercy. Beg to be spared the sting of His wrath! For He will not tolerate transgression. He will not abide deception. There are things you should never contemplate. And there are things you should do to salvage your soul. Things you should avoid like the child avoids the father."

The fire leaped and flared and, through the veil of flame that cloaked Lucretia in its fury, there appeared a vision. A vision Graziella wished to forget. For there before her, embodied in the conflagration that was Lucretia, appeared her father, his face twisted into a horrid grimace. Without warning, he pounced at her, held her so she could not escape and groped at places she had never before contemplated. Unable to move, unable to free herself, unable to unleash the scream that yearned to escape from her innocent lips, she stood paralyzed and endured what she would ever wish to erase from her soul.

And then the fire ceased. The vision disappeared. The horror dissipated. And in its place stood Lucretia, her long, bony fingers gripping the crucifix that dangled by her side, her eye as hard and icy as it had been before, as if *he* had instilled in her all *his* eternal wrath. Releasing the beads from her hand, she swatted Graziella with the back of her hand. Once. Twice. Three times. Then, without a word, she left the room and quietly shut the door behind her.

All this I watched, concealed in the very fire that had engulfed Lucretia, as the crucifix, dangling by her side, prevented me from stepping in. How my heart melted! How my pride ached, burned to the very core of my being! As Graziella emerged from Lucretia's spell, I longed to hold her in my arms. To embrace her as fire embraces wood. Instead, all I could do was curse the day I was created. To curse *him*, over and over. *he* who had wrought me as I was. *he* who had condemned me to this life of unrelenting torment. *he* who had sent Lucretia to thwart my desires.

Unable to control myself, unable any longer to bear the torture I had endured for eternity, I cried out—once again—a cry so filled with anguish, so loud, so imbued with self-pity, so filled with unrelenting rage that

the building shook. Again, the floors rattled. Again, the walls quaked. Again, Graziella—my sweet, sweet Graziella—the one who had unknowingly captured my heart—watched in horror as the world around her swiftly disintegrated.

Chapter 16

Several days went by. Several days in which Graziella lay aswoon in Lucretia's bleak chamber. Several days surrendered to a feverish delirium, tossing about on that rigid bed in endless fits of restlessness. For during that maelstrom of destruction that I had engendered, in a wanton moment of inconsolable despair, Graziella had taken ill—taken by a fit of fright and anguish as the room came tumbling down about her, as the walls shook and the ceilings crumbled and the floors buckled until nothing could stand aright. Taken by a sudden draft that swiftly penetrated that wretched chamber, an unmistaken chill, a cold sepulchral iciness that swallowed the abbey in its violent wake.

As if destruction had not already rendered itself supreme in that forsaken abbey!

Several days, several weeks passed, and Lucretia tended to Graziella, viciously, erratically—even, dare I say, tenderly—at times bathing her forehead with a cool cloth dipped in water and herbs, at others, flagellating her tender flesh with a leather knout she kept hidden beneath her wretched bed. Back and forth, back and forth, nursing, torturing, all the while praying vehemently, all the while contemplating, through the clouded orb of her evil eye, the helpless waif who lay, insensible, at her mercy.

Several weeks, several fortnights, and Father Francesco, ever vigilant against Lucretia's overzealous ways, wary of her severe disposition, convinced of her incapacity for compassion and her vast facility for retribution, constantly came and went, looking in on Graziella, anointing her forehead with holy oils, praying and chanting and exercising every aspect of his sacred office, soliciting *him* in every possible way to spare her from death, all the while keeping a careful eye on Graziella's fanatical keeper who had carefully hidden her wounds beneath a thick white shroud—under the guise of keeping her warm and comfortable.

Father Francesco, fueled by feelings I kept alive in his tenuous heart, watched over her like he had watched over no other in his former life. Little did he know that she meant more to me alive, more, now, than she ever would if she suddenly passed into the realms of death. For if she parted from this world before I had had a chance to stake my claim, she would be forever beyond my reach.

Months went by, and Graziella remained in that miserable state, and Lucretia, impelled by my silent whispers, fed her and bathed her and administered whatever ministrations she could conjure, until her resistance got the better of her, and her face, rippling, as her conscience struggled between *him* and me, transformed once again, and she reverted anew to her relentless tortures.

And all the while, Graziella lay delirious: tossing and turning, languishing, bleeding, withering away except for a slight protrusion which slowly swelled in her abdomen, growing gradually week by week, which Father Francesco noticed one day, through the fold of cotton that covered her. And when he realized what it was—when he remembered poor Perdita and all the others who had suffered under Lucretia's hands—he tried to conceal it, for he knew that Lucretia's heartless punishments would only increase as soon as she observed. And all the while I whispered into that wicked nun's ear, all the while, trying my best to blind her from the truth that burgeoned gradually before her.

Imagine! Me! Filling Lucretia's mind with thoughts of pity and sorrow! Tempting her with feelings of love and compassion! But once again, *he* was interfering. Once again, *he* was standing in my way, trying to prevent me from getting my due. So I turned, out of desperation, to other methods, and slowly, the thick rigid lines on Lucretia's forehead transformed. Gradually, her face began to soften: the distant look in her opaque eye disappeared as the other reemerged; slowly, her shrunken mouth began to blossom and relax; her face glowed with warmth. And soon, she returned to her former self. Soon, she was transformed into the novice she had once been, the novice who had joyfully joined the abbey, young and innocent and devoid of the evil I had so carefully implanted deep inside her.

Father Francesco noticed. Father Francesco, who I had summoned back from the dead—summoned to protect Graziella—observed Lucretia return to the flower of her youth and, at once, his attentions turned to her, at once, the memories reappeared and his feelings for Graziella dissipated. And soon Lucretia—Sister Lucretia—set her softened gaze upon his, leaving Graziella solely for my pleasure.

And to help with this metamorphosis, to assist with the fiction I was creating for all to believe, I regenerated that shattered abbey, replaced every stone, every beam, every object that had been dislodged, back to its rightful place so that the abbey was restored to its solemn glory, peopled it with the nuns and monks whose lives, like Father Francesco's, were resurrected from their somber graves.

But not everything can be rectified, nor its reality neglected, forgotten, forged into something other than what it is. Nothing returns to its former glory, no matter the powers we may have, no matter how we try. For throughout all of this, the shadowy creature who had frightened Graziella upon her arrival at the abbey, came and went. Outside Sister Lucretia's window, it lurked. Outside, in the darkness and the light. Imperceptible almost, yet distinctly present. Peering into the room through the window. Leering at Graziella. Spying on

Sister Lucretia. Keeping its eyes on Father Francesco as he went about his priestly duties. And though they pretended not to know—denied, even, its existence—though they chose to forget what could not be forgotten, they felt its presence. And though they ignored it, its existence weighed on their conscience, anchored in their guilt, down to the very depths of their souls. And every act, every breath they took, every gentle caress they lay on Graziella's feverish forehead, reminded them of its existence. For they knew that its wild eyes would forever stalk them wherever they were.

Chapter 17

Eventually, Graziella awoke, as if from a dream, awoke to a reality that was more dreamlike than her slumbers had been. Awoke, and her memories washed into a muddle of illusion and reality as the room slowly came into focus and the horrors of the abbey where she was imprisoned gradually faded into the tender arms of amnesia.

Before her loomed the specters of a priest and a nun, materializing as if life itself were a vague manifestation of something not quite real, elusive figments hovering tentatively in a room that was now devoid of devastation, speaking in low, intangible tones as if speech itself were a mere wisp of sound.

"We have brought her back, Sister Lucretia."

The words emerged as if from nowhere, arose like a fragile whisper come from the shadows. Graziella struggled to make sense of the echoes that came and went as if on their own, tried to perceive what her eyes could barely see, until she was finally able to tilt her heavy head and lift her weakened hand, look about and comprehend the substance of her tenuous surroundings.

"Yes, praise be to God, Father. Pray keep watch, while I bring another cloth to bathe her forehead."

Graziella gazed, bewildered, as the nun, whose face glowed in an aura of kindness, vanished from her muted vision, as the priest, who gently anointed her with holy oils, solemnly muttered prayers that imbued the room with a soothing hum and filled her with comfort, calmed her soul and allowed her to forget, for the moment, the horrors she had recently witnessed.

And I—I stood there, hidden as always, with an insatiable sense of joy as the plan I had wrought slowly took hold, for Graziella emerged from unconsciousness, emerged like a newborn child that had not yet experienced the sufferings of life, a child that could not yet comprehend the dangers that lay before her. And that goodly priest—that kindly nun—having now been reborn, having been brought back, forged from the remnants of their previous lives by my unquenchable will—having been returned to their former unblemished selves!—were unknowingly doing my bidding. For I had recreated them, molded them into the mindless effigies they had become. I guided them in every action they performed, fed them every word that they spoke. All in defiance of *him*!

Can you blame me for what I had done? Can you not understand? As you consider my plight, can you not take pity on me? Is your heart so hardened against me, so obdurate, so fully implacable that you would have no mercy, no sympathy even for one such as me? Not even one grain of consolation? Are you then so utterly heartless? Like *him* who, in utter and unappeasable wrath, condemned me ruthlessly to an eternity of utter loneliness? Are you not able to fathom the torture that I have endured since the very dawn of creation!

Here before me, lying innocently on a bed meant solely for the contrite, for those wedded to *him*, was my chance for love—unadulterated love—for tenderness, for compassion, for respite from the perpetuity of torment my existence had become. Would you then be so utterly cruel as to deny me this fleeting chance of relief?

Graziella would be mine. At all costs. Despite what *he* wanted! Despite what you or anyone in this accursed world might think! She would comfort me in my need. Perhaps, even, ease my temper, assuage my anger, alleviate the hatred that had been so skillfully instilled in me. And damn all those who dared to stand in my way!

Graziella sighed. She stirred. She grasped the rosary that had been coiled through her precious fingers. She struggled with the image of Father Francesco hovering before her—the kind, loving priest—and the horrid images that slowly began to rise up again from memory—images that lurked in the recesses of her mind and taunted her with their unrelenting persistence. And I gazed with untold tenderness—a tenderness I had never before experienced—as terror once again erupted within her fearful brown eyes. For despite the transformation I had carefully wrought to the room in which she lay, despite the soothing veils of Lethe with which I had swaddled her restless mind, the memories slowly emerged into view. And that rosary—that twisted string of useless beads Lucretia had looped through her slender fingers—could not possibly bring her comfort. Nor could the book which Father Francesco had set on the bed beside her. Nor could the solemn, hopeless prayers he blindly recited. How could they defy me with these wretched acts! How could they resist my will!

And so the ghastly images resurfaced, slowly burst into a flare of panic that began to take hold, a spell of utter fear, a spasm of that base instinct for survival that every animal possesses. And Graziella began to thrash about, wildly, inconsolably, on that most miserable of beds, as the memories became more vivid than reality and submerged all feelings of well-being.

How could I bear this! How could I watch as she suffered so! As she struggled with the haunted reminders of the terror she had been through! As Father Francesco, lost in the futile repetition of worthless prayers, remained oblivious to her suffering!

It was then that I made my move. At last, I knew my chance had come. Slowly, ever so softly, I came out from the shadows. Gradually, I appeared—first, a cloven foot, then a misshapen leg, charred and blackened by the fires of iniquity, then a wing, once so white and pure, once so capable of soaring high through the heavens, now twisted and sinister-looking, weighed down by an eternity of hatred and suffering. And finally, my wretched face—those sallow orbs casting a sickly pall throughout that miserable room. And the smile—the hideous smile!—once so comely, once so irresistible, now a mere maw of jagged teeth and rotten skin.

I inched my way toward her—quietly, stealthily. I made not a sound, cast not a shadow. So she would not notice—not yet, not yet! So Father Francesco, who was now my shield, would not stir. Lest he be roused from his meditations. Lest too much too soon would send Graziella into another swoon of terror from which even I would be unable to retrieve her.

Little by little, inch by inch, I came forward, as Father Francesco prayed, as Graziella broke into a fierce sweat, as her head thrashed relentlessly back and forth, back and forth, on that horrid bed upon which she lay. When suddenly she saw me. Suddenly, her eyes bulged and her expression twisted and she let out a scream that echoed through the halls of that derelict abbey. The abbey I had built! The one I had so thoroughly destroyed! The one I had recreated!

I tried to calm her, to assuage her fear. I smiled, gently, as anyone would do—but what effect would a smile like mine generate but to instill more fear? I lifted my wings—softly, lovingly, like a bird protecting its young. I reached out with my disfigured hand—my misshapen claws. But each movement, each gesture, each attempt at consolation, served only to heighten her horror, to increase her agitation, to make her scream as if screaming were the sole purpose of her being.

Graziella looked pleadingly toward Father Francesco, begging for help, but he was fully blind to my presence, fully blind to her need, for he continued to pray, unfazed, oblivious to her pleas, as if lost in a world that was all his own.

Still, I proceeded—persisted with an ardor that would make any man jealous, reaching out with my gnarled fingers, pleading with every ounce of my wretched soul for a chance—an improbable chance that she could love me as I loved her. As I deserved! And yet, she persisted in rejecting me, persisted in her stubborn refusal of my tender intentions.

Standing beside her miserable bed, I observed her, ripe with fear, wilting from weakness. I leaned over, reached as slowly and gently as I could, but just as I was about to swaddle her up into the folds of my wretched wings, just as I was about to whisk her away from all the horror that had become her life, carry her off to my den where she would be forever safe—where she would be my queen!—Sister Lucretia returned, entered the room with the damp cloth she had gone to retrieve. And dangling by her side, swaying with each step as she walked toward Graziella—was that cursed crucifix. A cross with *him* hung miserably upon it, a talisman for all who wished to be in *his* good graces. All, except for me!

I cowered in fear. I covered my eyes with my wretched wings. I let out a howl that filled the halls with my anger—a howl that manifested itself as a sudden squall—and retreated quickly back into the darkness and cursed all and sundry in that miserable, forsaken place.

Chapter 18

It was, in the end, my fault—a result of my proceeding too slowly, too cautiously, too softly, of initiating my intentions in such an elusive way that Graziella would somehow accept my attempts at wooing her, enticing her, loving her. So that—let's face it—she would not be frightened out of life when one so ghastly in appearance as I approached her despite my sincerest intentions. No, I had reasoned. It had to be gradual. I had to be gentle. I had to do things in such a way that, eventually, Graziella would accept me. And—dare I say?—love me. Adore me. For how else could one such as I—unsightly, wicked by repute, misunderstood due to the unfair way I have forever been portrayed—expect to win over one so pure, so innocent as she? It was simply not to be. It was something that even I—*especially* I—should have understood. For who has ever had the courage to love me? Who has ever accepted me for who I am? Who has ever approached me with kindness, compassion, even simple consideration? Certainly not *him*! Certainly not *you* who, at the very thought of me, lurch for cover, cower in fear! Who instinctively sympathize with those like Graziella and tremble for their lives—for their very souls!—at every movement I make!

No, I should never have expected to win Graziella over in this way. I should not have pretended that there would be love at first and only sight. Oh, what foolish thoughts we sometimes invoke! What insipid beliefs we conjure when need pulls at our very essence in those moments when all we desire is a bit of respite from the depths of loneliness!

No, it was apparent now. I could not win over Graziella like any gentle lover would do: wooing and courting and showering her with attention. For that is not who I am. How could I possibly be! For *he* had not created me that way. No, *he* had created me to be an example of what one should *not* be. An example of utter misery and abjection to warn those such as you into being what *he* had intended. What *he demanded.* And I to suffer as a result! I to be the sacrificial lamb, the fallen angel—yes, angel!—whose agony would not be spared, whose black blood slowly, eternally, courses, drop by drop, through this infernal world: a lurid example for all that is not good in *his* wretched eyes!

But good intention sometimes breeds the unexpected. For misery and abject behavior, while scaring away some, quickly attract others, like decomposing flesh attracts an eager mass of maggots. Such is the world we inhabit. One is sacrificed so that others might live.

And so I immediately came to my senses. I realized I would have to resort to other means. If Graziella could not be mine through any honest endeavor—through a compromise of my very nature!—I would have to seek other ways. I would have to be true to myself and rely on schemes that I knew, from experience, would work best.

Graziella lay convalescent in that bleak room—an inhospitable cell despite the restoration I had recently rendered—and I watched from the dark crevices of my misery and waited for a chance to assert my will as I cursed the moment I had spied her running through that dreary forest.

Lucretia—defiant to my wishes, defiant to my very intention for her spurious reincarnation—now good, now holy—the wicked Sister Lucretia, the one who had long ago been despoiled in the sacristy when Father Francesco, under my guidance, coaxed her into temptation—remained adamant now in her newly revivified role as the meek nun, forgetting, or ignoring, the one who was responsible for her rekindled existence. Adamant, she resisted my newly contrived temptations with fervor and fortitude and, contrary to my commands, tended, instead, to Graziella night and day with the sole intention of protecting her from me. And Father Francesco, who I had reawakened to be just as he had been before—whose very goodness I needed to realize my plan!—remained lost in solemn intonations, uttering prayers and benedictions and watching over Graziella as her stolid guardian and protector.

Days passed—days and nights in which I remained anguished, yet vigilant—and Graziella faded and recovered, faded and recovered, moving in and out between consciousness and insensibility. As the days turned into weeks, she slowly regained her strength. Gradually, Sister Lucretia began to take her from her room, supporting her, guiding her as they treaded carefully down the long, narrow corridors, out into the open where the sun and the ocean air and the sound of the sea would assist in her slow recovery.

For the abbey, flanked by the forest on one side, faced the ocean on the other, and was situated atop a cliff that served as protection from sudden squalls and stormy seas. And as an impediment for those desperate souls whose only wish was to escape.

On sunny days, a gentle breeze grazed the barren rocks, swept across the scraggly moor that led to the abbey whose crumbling belfry overlooked the gray, foaming deep. On stormy nights, when winter ravaged what life was left in its frigid tempests, the sullen sound of the wind whistled a foreboding dirge to those who dared to risk the gloom of the moonless night. And here and there, sunken in the sand, appeared the remains of those who had tried to flee—skeletal relics, hidden among rocks, concealed partially by tumbleweed, buried under tufts of wild grass and sand—a solemn paean to those whose fate had already been written.

Here, Lucretia brought her charge, skirting skulls and rushing past broken bones. Here, Graziella, oblivious to all, continued to recover, breathing in the salt air, absorbing the life-giving rays of the sun, once again forgetting the horrors she had witnessed in that forlorn abbey, unaware of the horror that yet surrounded her. Here, I watched and waited, yearned patiently for the right moment to make my move, tried and failed to tempt Lucretia to surrender Graziella to my burning clutches. Defiant, she continued to resist me with every ounce of her soul. And that cross—that sinister crucifix!—would at once turn its wretched face toward mine, as if it had a life of its own, and drive me away with all its horrid might.

And all the time, that shadowy form—that abominable creature—lurking in the distance. Watching with stealthy eyes. Stalking Graziella with intentions that even I could not surmise. Hidden behind scrub and dune, staring and waiting as Sister Lucretia helped her down the sloping hill, down to the mossy cliffs where the wash of the waves arose and mesmerized her into a state of quietude.

And then, one day, good fortune came my way. Good fortune, that is, if one considers disaster something that bodes fairly. Graziella was sitting near the edge of the sea cliff, mesmerized by the sound of the rolling waves, soothed by a pleasant breeze stroking her soft cheeks, while Lucretia, immersed in her breviary, her fingers mindlessly rubbing the beads on her worn rosary, sat beside her, transfixed in prayer, mindless of her surroundings.

Immediately, I went to work. Gently, faintly, I whispered in Graziella's ear. So quietly, so tenderly, that it could have been the mere sound of the ocean or the hushed quiver of the wind as it brushed against her skin and caressed her with its elusive touch, its resonance beguiling her, its soft fingers stroking her, enfolding her in a soft cocoon of warmth, embracing her and summoning her to follow in its path—to follow and land in my burning arms.

Slowly, she stood up—tentatively, took one step, then another, and gradually approached, each foot carefully assessing its precarious hold, her arms outstretched, as if sleepwalking, her eyes spellbound as if engulfed in a trance whose grip was inescapable. And I, all the while, whispering—"Graziella, Graziella." The sound of my voice so delicate. So inviting. "Graziella." So mellifluous. So hypnotic. So inescapable!

At last, Graziella was within my grasp. Under my influence. Swayed by my beguiling words. Aroused by the soothing, irresistible rush of sensation that spread through her consciousness—the waves crashing against rock, the seagulls crying out, the warm breeze caressing every inch of her body. And my voice—gentle, compelling, irresistible.

And then it happened. Of a sudden. Without even my awareness or intention, for I was so enthralled with her every movement, with her newly awakened desire to be with me, that I did not notice, did not even suspect. For Graziella took one step too far—one last precarious footstep before she reached my arms—and, with a sudden scream, slipped off the cragged edge—for I was hovering before her, hovering mindlessly in the heights of a forbidden love to which I had been held captive—and tumbled from that rocky precipice toward the hungry chasm of the sea.

Sister Lucretia, summoned from her prayers by Graziella's calls, cried out for help, cried out so loud that her voice echoed across the vast moor and reached Father Francesco who came rushing down the hill, rushing from the abbey as if he, himself, were on fire.

Fortunately, for Graziella, there was a protrusion of rock not far below the edge of the cliff, a narrow flange on which she landed and now, awakening from my spell and hearing the voices of those who came running to rescue her, reached up with her arms—reached up in fear—and with the help of Father Francesco and Sister Lucretia, was extricated from that calamitous situation and escorted back to the abbey where she lay in her bed in yet another swoon.

And the creature rushed toward the sea and lumbered like the cretin that he was and marked the spot where disaster had struck—marked the spot with a glance of his yellow eyes—and he let out a sound that no known beast or mortal could possibly make.

Chapter 19

How could I have been so careless? How could I have imperiled the one I most wanted to possess? Yes, in death she would have been mine—eternally mine. If I had played my cards right. If I had claimed her soul before *he* did. But to what end? For what purpose? To feed my pride? So that I could boast to *him* of yet another conquest? No, I had to earn her—to win her unmitigated devotion through every possible endeavor. She had to come to me of her own free will. Otherwise, I would be deceiving myself, for the love of a woman is something that cannot so easily be attained—and it was her love, her unwavering fidelity to me, that I craved. Graziella had to come willingly. With full consent. With full knowledge of who I was. Who I *am*! Only then would I be satisfied.

So once again, I set to work, searching for a portal into her soul. I lurked quietly about the desolate halls of the abbey and observed everyone who inhabited those sorry walls, seeking someone who could aid me in my pursuit. Those I had brought back from the dead and those who stood firm against my presence, who spurned me, who resisted my each and every overture. As if without me they would have been able to draw even one meager breath!

And for once, I felt like *him*. Felt the sting of knowing that *my* subjects had the tenacity to defy me. To pretend that, without me, their presence in this abbey—their resurrected existence—would even be possible!

Each night, I watched as Sister Lucretia tended to her devotions, kneeling beside her sputtering candle, grasping that ghastly crucifix between her fingers as she prayed. Each morning, in the pit of dawn, I spied as Father Francesco, ever so gentle, ever so kind, conducted mass in the chapel, tended to his lifeless flock of worshipers and kept a wary eye out for mischief and evil. And I gazed, ever so keenly, almost unable to control myself, upon Graziella, whose health was now fully restored—whose body, once again, attained its youthful blush, who now showed fully that which was growing inside her. And yet, her appearance belied the terror that had been buried in the thick folds of her consciousness.

Then, one night, as the moon struggled to maintain its steady glow, as the clouds thickened with increasing force and raced across the turbid sky, a furious storm broke out. It was the kind of storm that takes one by surprise—swift and unexpected—the kind that shakes the earth and sets a trembling in the hearts of men.

The winds blew with furious rage. Lightning lit up the sky with an uncertain glow. Thunder rocked the abbey with a force that even the dead, lying within their cold, eternal crypts, could not ignore.

It so happened that the congregation was assembled in the chapel at the time, gathered in prayer amidst what had once been ruin and rubble, amidst what I had since restored—the chandelier that lay fallen behind the altar now set aright; the splintered statues fully restored; the shattered stained-glass windows, intact and pulsing with each sliver of lightning.

Father Francesco stood before the assembly, prevailed despite the rain and wind which battered the abbey. Leading that congregation of moribund souls in the evening nocturnes, he prayed, and the congregants all responded in monotonous tones that could barely be heard above the clamor of thunder as the candles flickered and the wind slithered through unsealed crevices.

Suddenly, the candles died, all at once—snuffed out in an instance of abrupt wind—and the only light in that suddenly darkened chamber came from the lightning that illuminated the chapel with increasing intensity. Panic ensued as each one of those lifeless souls forsook their penance and sought solace from the raging storm. Struggling to escape from the narrow pews and groping through the blinding shadows, they stumbled over each other and strove to seek shelter from the fear raging in their hollow hearts.

I laughed as I watched them—dead souls who had experienced the jaws of death, now seeking escape from a world they had never wished to leave. And then there was Graziella who attempted to evade their desperate attempts to scramble past her but ended up on the ground as panic turned into sheer terror.

I cried out at the sight of her fallen on the ground, as the others trampled her in their fright—a cry so loud and fearsome that each of them froze on the spot. Froze in fear, though, for all they knew, it could have been the incessant yowling of wind or the angry growling of thunder. And then, through the silence that ensued, through the stillness that suddenly seized the abbey, I approached her, clearing a path through the darkness, shoving aside anyone who stood in my way. As I stooped down to lift her in my lustful arms, to swaddle her under my wanton wings, a flash of lightening, so bright, so intense, ignited the room, and Graziella, seeing me hovering above her, let out a scream so piercing that even the dead, lying lifeless below in the catacombs, quaked in their time-worn shrouds.

I lifted her up and swept her away. Swept her away under my hungry wings, trying to reassure her with a look on my wretched face that she would never come to harm. That she would always be mine!

But such is the way of the world—that good intentions, belied by untoward appearances, can never be conveyed. And try as I might, she squirmed in my arms, resisted me with all her heart and soul, as I swooped through the murky corridors and bore her down to my anxious den.

Chapter 20

Yes, I swept her away, limp and delirious in my fiery arms. Swooped through that cursed abbey, cradling her under my burning wings, flew through the abandoned hallways, down the twisted corridors where those tortured ghosts perpetually roamed, searching in vain for their unclaimed souls. Like a predator with its prey, I rushed through the shriveled gardens, clutching Graziella between my feverish claws, tore through the desiccated grounds, overcome by weed and insect, and descended into the dark, forbidden passageways that led to the crypts and the unsealed tombs covered in the dust of those who longed to rest, of those who but merely rot in their eternal misery.

Arriving at the chamber where Lucretia, under my tutelage, had done her wicked deeds, I threw open the door, lit the torches with a flash of my eye and set Graziella gently atop the very tomb where my acolyte's victims had met their final days.

And then I retreated, disappeared into the shadows, into the dark recesses of a dungeon where yet untold deeds had been done. Retreated and waited for my cherished one—my queen!—to rustle from beneath her fearsome slumbers—to awaken and surrender at last to my unquenched desire.

But I was not alone. Soon the faint sounds of moaning arose from the dim corners of the chamber—laments as faint as the last waning breaths of a sacrificial offer. And then the gradual swelling of whimpers and cries emerged—a crescendo of wailing voices seeking refuge from the pit of pain into which they had been forever plunged. Voices—abandoned and hopeless—awakening, seeking the soothing balm of salvation, the salve of pity that had been denied them in life and that was never to be found in the hellish hollows of death.

I watched as they appeared—spirits leaching through the thick, wooden portal that had stood as a shield for those who dared not enter when they were alive. They seeped through the stone walls, oozed like some unholy substance, materializing, rising up from the unhallowed earth in which they had been cruelly interred, and from the very tomb where Graziella lay unawares, unconscious of the world of wailing and woe that now surrounded her.

There they convened. The ghosts of women and their unborn children: those who had been mercilessly tortured and those whose premature bodies had been ripped from the womb. Anxious specters. Phantoms of men and women whose lives had not been spared and who now encircled Graziella in their ghostly torment.

They reached out to her with rotten limbs and haunted eyes. Their voices, filled with pain, echoed throughout that macabre chamber and probed the very depths of Graziella's as yet unlost soul.

And then she awoke, instantly sensed her gruesome surroundings—the cold, clammy ectoplasm that stroked her trembling flesh, that made her shiver such that she could not emit even one sound though her face was contorted in fear.

I let out a roar that should have frightened the strongest of souls, but those heartless spirits resisted my rage and sought me out from the hollows of their anguished eyes. Condemned to an eternity of torture, hardened by a world in which pain no longer mattered, they stood in defiance of my power—in defiance of the one to whom they were eternally bound, to whom they bowed down in constant worship as the fires of hell crackled all about them.

I leapt out of the shadows. I entered their swirling ring of foul flesh and tortured spirit, tried to shield Graziella from their wicked stares as the echo of their moans penetrated the chamber. Defiant, they tightened their circle as if to shield her from me—from the one who adored her, from the one who would not let one monstrous finger touch her delicate body.

And then, at last, that blessed sound—the rustling of that ruthless nun who, having heard the unearthly commotion, had suddenly awakened to the unmerciful knowledge she had once been privy to. Returning to her evil ways, shedding the veil of innocence that had once again enveloped her flesh, she rushed through the crypts, shedding that wretched crucifix along the way. And with a flourish of pure evil, Sister Lucretia—my apprentice, my savior!—burst into the room.

"Depart!" she cried. "Depart and leave the girl. There's nothing you can do for her now."

She looked straight through them—stared with a countenance that would have withered the trees had there been any in that desolate chamber. And one by one they scattered—retreated into the shadows from whence they had come, returning, once again, to their world of pain and torture, forsaking the chamber and the one living soul they had endeavored to save.

Lucretia turned her eye toward me—that singular orb that graced her face that had once again assumed its grisly look—turned and nodded, as she glanced toward Graziella, with a smile that was as ghastly and beautiful as the urgent sting of a black widow.

And then she left the room, slammed the door with a thud. At last, I was alone! Alone, to do as I pleased. Alone, with the one who would soon be crowned my queen. Who I would anoint and initiate into the wicked ways of hell.

But it was then that the shadow—the beast that had stalked Graziella since her arrival—came forth, lumbered lugubriously into that hellish chamber and stood, insolently drooling over Graziella who, throughout the commotion, had fallen again into a thankful faint.

"Begone!" I cried.

But he ignored my command. He dismissed the roar that arose from my miserable soul. He resisted the contempt and hatred that had been instilled in me from the day I had been rendered into this world, defied every threat I could conjure, and I knew then that he had the power to challenge me like no other, to withstand whatever I threw in his way. For he was of my own flesh, of my own foul loins—a result of the union between me and Lucretia—and no matter what I did, he would prevail as his evil mother had prevailed, as, indeed, I had prevailed since the dawn of creation.

I stepped forward, pounced at him as anyone would do when threatened, lashed out, released the full force of my fury until that chamber roared with the sting of my anger. And still he stared at me, dumb and adamant, stared with his tiny yellow eyes until, at last, unable to withstand my fury, he succumbed, cowered into a ball of fear and lumbered off into his world of loneliness and sorrow.

Graziella and I were alone now. Completely alone. At last! I would have her now. She would be mine. There she lay, unconscious, awaiting my embrace, waiting, unknowingly, for the consummation of her fate.

Ready to be baptized into the world of evil.

Chapter 21

I won't relate all the delicate details, though I know your heart hungers to hear. I won't describe how I tasted of Graziella's earthly beauty in that most unearthly of places, how I plunged into the depths of her passion—a passion no woman has ever known—how I made her flesh tremble with yearning, tempted her in ways no mortal ever could. She was there and I took. But I gave as well. Gave all that was in me, all that had been kept imprisoned in this grotesque shell since that fatal day I was forced into this wretched life. And she—still ensconced in a lovely swoon of amnesia, craving warmth and comfort on that cold, hard crypt, her face sweetly contorted into a twist of terror—struggled and resisted, and at last surrendered to my irrepressible passion.

When it was over, I sent a cry of joy racing through that abbey as I lifted myself up, still unsatiated, and stood beside her—stood and watched as Graziella, who was now fully in my possession, drifted back into a miasma of forgetfulness, her soft skin rippling, as frightful fits of memory pierced her blissful cloud of unconsciousness.

†

After that, the abbey returned to normal. Normal, that is, for a place that did not fit the usual mode of normality.

Lucretia and her newly resurrected flock returned to what work they had carried out long before they had entered the bowels of the earth—gathering honey, milking cows, churning cheese and butter; attending chapel at the appointed hours and keeping a watchful eye out for behavior that was not in keeping with the stringent rules they purported to follow. A prayer missed or a misspoken benediction became the cause for severe rebuke. A word uttered when silence was required, a furtive glance when glance was not permitted, resulted in punishment—castigation at first; thereafter, flagellation, conducted under that stern Mother Superior's ever-vigilant eye. All on flesh that had once rested in the grave, now newly revived, now stinging in the most vibrant of ways.

But this was no flock of ordinary nuns, rendered from innocence and gathered in the guise of prayer. For beneath the patina of goodness that emanated was a layer of evil that percolated unseen and manifested itself in between gestures of sanctity. For all that was executed was done in devotion to me.

Father Francesco, meanwhile, spent his days copying scripture in a hand so controlled and so beautiful that the words seemed to float before one's eyes. Yet the words he wrote were not the words he had ever wished to replicate. And in between calligraphic exercises and contemplations to ease the heart, he mindlessly chanted his prayers in the privacy of his cell—prayers that contained whispers of ungodliness—and led his worshippers in matins and vespers and all the other devotions required of those poor lifeless souls.

But beyond these worldly deeds, executed in the most precise manner, those lifeless zombies—flesh and bone and blood resuscitated from the dank dust from which I had awakened them—the dank dust that had encrusted their crypts since their departure from this unforgiving world—roamed about: mere shells with no substance, mere cavities with no spirit. For their souls remained in the realms of the underworld—in the regions which I alone commanded.

And then there was Lucretia whose strong will could not be fully broken. Who worshipped me from the deep pit of her twisted soul yet yearned for *him* who she equally adored. Whose malice abounded without constraint, as she did my bidding, all the while seeking solace in the mercy of *one* who had not done half of what I had done for her. Sister Lucretia: the woman I wished to fully conquer. Who teased me with her devotion and spurned me with her disdain.

The abbey itself gradually returned to a state of disrepair. The walls soon crumbled. The corridors, just recently clean and tidy, with no sign of disorder or destruction, became once again a panoply of disarray. The gardens, though never quite restored to their former verdant splendor, were now more rampant with rot and weed. And the chapel—the center of that once sanctimonious community—again fell into utter decay—the altar upturned, the statues moldering upon their shattered platforms. And the stained-glass windows—once so subdued, so pure that the chamber itself seemed almost an ethereal haven for those seeking solace—now transformed into a web of cracks and slivers, allowing light and wind and rain to bleed into that derelict chamber. As for that massive crucifix— that horrid symbol of *he* who has stood brazenly against me—though in its proper place, affixed high above the altar, it still overlooked the congregation, gathered for my adulation. But it was now turned on its head and shrouded in a black crepe. For they came now, all and one, to pray to *me*. To worship *me*. To adore *me*!

Throughout all the daily comings and goings— throughout the deeds that were done, the sins that were committed—not one word was said about Graziella. It was as if she had never set foot in the abbey. As if the memory of her presence had been erased from their souls, leaving her solely for me. You might say she was my prisoner. But for me, she was the empress of my kingdom. I kept her in that dungeon for my pleasure, but I elevated her to a station she would never have known before. She was a secret. *My* secret. The secret of an abbey defiled, created in my image. Kept hidden from all. And even *he* could not keep her from me. Even *he* could no longer save her.

A secret to all except for Lucretia who continued to do my bidding, blindly, willingly, devoutly, in between bouts of devotion to *him*. Every night, when the nuns were interred in their cells, when Father Francesco was entangled in his twisted prayers—she would sneak down into the crypts, bringing Graziella food and wine, providing her with the necessities that allowed for her survival. Lucretia worshipped me, though she would never admit it, more than she worshipped *him*, and she obeyed me like no other and did what I commanded no matter what the task.

Except for those times when she grasped that infernal breviary in between her bony hands—grasped it and held it tight against her chest as if she were holding on to something that might be snatched from her. And then her face would transform from the wicked woman that she was to the pure angel of innocence she had once been—an angel she wished so much to become once again.

And so it is, even now. Sister Lucretia obeys my orders. When she is in her room, late at night, in the midst of contemplation, I call and Lucretia listens. I command and Lucretia obeys. I suggest and Lucretia acts without hesitation. Though the one thing I have demanded of her, she has refused. Sister Lucretia, the once virtuous nun, refuses to become my queen, despite our intimacies. Refuses to give to me what she has reserved for *him*. And though Graziella remains my chosen one, the one whose sweet torturous existence rends my soul, it is Lucretia whom I wish to conquer. Sister Lucretia. Whose wickedness conforms to my evil nature. Graziella, perhaps, could tame me. Satisfy me. Make me forget an eternity of disdain and torture. But it is Lucretia whose soul I wish to make utterly mine.

Chapter 22

But let us return to Graziella. The unwilling prisoner of my heart. Languishing in that cold, dark chamber. Shackled to an ancient stone crypt, as her body and soul were now forever chained to mine. Her only companions the rats and insects that brushed against her in their search for nourishment. Her only source of light the torches that burned eternally on those dank walls. Her only solace the shadows, cast from the constant flickers of their feverish flames—the only indication that time was not standing still.

And the creature, who lurked in the shadows, who watched over her constantly, panting and leering and yearning for something I refused to let him have.

When she first awoke from her stupor—from that night of unsurpassed joy that she could barely comprehend—that she could scarcely remember—Graziella opened her languid eyes, looked around—stunned, dazed, still immersed in a state of dream and amnesia. Gradually, her senses returned. Gradually, she began to see, to understand and to regret. Regret the day she had entered that forest. Regret the day she had taken refuge in an abbey whose very aura had cast a sense of gloom. And then the tears. The sobs. The cries for help that fell on the ears of no one but the dead who were ever present. And the creature, whose wit was too dim to comprehend.

My heart ached as I watched this poor creature—the one whose love I had yet to fully conquer—surrender to fear and despair. Such sweet torture! Such exquisite lamentation coming from the depths of vulnerability. How could I watch unmoved as she thrashed about, the chains grating against the cold stone? The feeling I had, as her sobs faded into faint echoes, caused even my blackest of hearts to beat faster than it should. I stirred in the shadows, attempted to once again reveal myself, but each step I took caused her to jump; each rustling, as I emerged from the darkness, caused her to shrink in horror. So I held myself back, tried to stifle every sound I made, though every movement, every muffled breath from my sulfurous lungs, manifested itself in ways that sent shivers down her delicate spine.

And so I enlisted Sister Lucretia to assist with my keep. Each day, when she came, bearing bread and wine—a nibble of something more substantial whenever possible—she would comfort her, as best she could. Quietly. Soothingly. Until, without warning, on a righteous whim, she would rebuke her in a fashion that sent Graziella into a state of terror.

"Child. You must eat or you will waste away," she would gently say.

And silently, Graziella would refuse the sustenance she was offered, then break into a whimper which would cause Sister Lucretia's patience to wither and die. Swiftly, patience was replaced by anger, and Sister Lucretia's face would swell into a welt of wickedness, her fist tightening into a mound of rage, and her voice would rise to a pitch that would pierce the dark chamber.

Graziella would quickly turn her face, cower and curl up, covering her ears and her head with her tattered shawl, expecting the sting of Sister Lucretia's tongue, fearing the nip of her leather lash.

One day, when the gnaw of hunger was especially sharp and Sister Lucretia appeared especially kind, she took a bite of stale bread and a sip of rancid wine and, carefully assessing the woman looming above her, asked softly: "Why am I here?"

Sister Lucretia's mild demeanor swiftly changed. Her face hardened into a brittle mask, her nostrils flared and her voice rose to a pitch that no ordinary mortal would be capable of.

"Because you are evil," she answered. "Because God does not take pity on one like you. Why do you think he led you here? To punish you. To prepare you for the retribution still to come."

And then, seizing a torch from the wall, she held it close to Graziella's face, waved it menacingly so that the heat of its flame singed the hair on her head.

"This is what you will feel. The flames will lick your flesh. Your skin will melt, only to return for more. Eternally! There shall be no mercy for one such as you who consorts with the devil and shows not one morsel of repentance."

And when Sister Lucretia's fury reached its peak of zealousness, Graziella would whimper, cry out, beg for mercy. Later, only later, when she understood that these acts only further provoked Sister Lucretia's vehement frenzy, she learned to turn her face, to refuse to speak, to ignore the flare of Lucretia's unsolaced soul. Silently, she would pray—pray to *him*—entreating *him* to foist some calamity upon Sister Lucretia—a pox of some sort or even sudden death—or that Sister Lucretia's anger would deflate somehow and she would return to normal.

Lucretia's zealousness knew no bounds. Her maniacal devotion to me—her irrepressible fervor for *him*—reached such a state that Graziella's hopelessness went from fear and despair to an acute state of numbness. Such was her condition that she neither ate nor drank, and she began to wither away and soon became deadened to her wretched solitude, craved it, even, over those brief uncertain visits from one who could not manage the loyalties she professed.

Chapter 23

Father Francesco continued to carry out his monastic duties as if nothing untoward had occurred, as if, having been brought back to life, he had not yet fully savored the foul entrails of death, for now, having been delivered from the depths of darkness, he behaved as if he had absolutely no gratitude, no debt to me, his dark savior.

Each dawn he would rise from the veils of sleep, as he had done before his death, each morning, mutter blindly from his breviary, prepare himself to perform his uncertain devotions in the chapel, ignoring me and all the temptations I continually inseminated into his venal mind. And then, having succeeded in repelling my lures and resisting my seductive charms, he would spend the day absorbed in his calligraphic arts and in the other duties that he replicated in order to keep the abbey running—in his feeble attempts to keep me at bay.

Like Lucretia, his body had been revived by my hot, sulfurous breath. Unlike her, his soul had never before been bound to my will, for there had been no covenant between us, not even an occasional capitulation. Try as I might, he squandered his days and nights in total devotion to *him*, rejecting each form of transgression I would softly suggest, even when he unknowingly transcribed words I secretly fed him—words that should never have been uttered by one such as he. His will was so unbreakable, so implacable, his faith in *him* so strong, that he was able to defy my advances at every turn. Even in those moments when he faltered—even now when his existence depended totally on my whims—he would quickly rise up and make amends. So adamant was his conviction that, each time he refused my entreaties, I would rush off enraged, return to the welcome arms of my squalid den.

And so his life—his *second* life—went on. A man whose soul belonged neither to this world nor the next, whose revivified existence was a direct result of my singular resolve. And yet, the imprint left by *him* on his spirit was so vivid, so indelible, that he declined to accommodate my presence, refused, despite my efforts, to bend to my will and abandon all efforts to worship *him*.

But there is always a chance. An opening. An opportunity. For eventually, each individual faces that moment of crisis when even the strongest conviction is put to the test. When what one believes in is suddenly set in such contrast with reality that confusion reigns and the very foundation of one's life—the very faith that one has carefully erected and buttressed—begins to crumble and, at last, topples abruptly into a mound of sand.

So while the lifeless shells around him went mindlessly about their daily duties, paying heed to neither *him* nor me, blindly attending devotions and the liturgical activities that had been indelibly engraved on their souls, and while Sister Lucretia struggled with her dedication to me and her misguided loyalty to *him*, Father Francesco persisted in his repudiation of my presence—prayed to *him* and *him* alone and ignored my every entreaty, as I patiently continued my quiet advances, waiting for that one weakness to bare itself for me to exploit.

And then it happened. That one flaw revealed itself, a flaw that was, in fact, a major hallmark of his righteous disposition, one which strengthened his convictions, one by which he lived his life—by which he was known—and which, now, was about to shatter his very faith in *him* and all that *he* stood for.

It began one evening, just before vespers were about to begin, after the daily meal which each one of those lifeless entities consumed though their frigid flesh did not require any sustenance. Father Francesco was exiting the refectory, quietly giving thanks to *him*, having just partaken of his meager meal, when he encountered Lucretia in the hallway clutching between her fingers a morsel of cheese and a sliver of bread which she quickly concealed in the folds of her habit. Lowering her eyes, as was the custom for the residents of the abbey, she proceeded down the corridor, acknowledging his presence with an almost imperceptible nod. Father

Francesco bowed in return, but his curiosity had been aroused, his suspicions baited, though he remained silent and continued to make his way toward the chapel as if nothing out of the ordinary had occurred.

This incident happened shortly after Graziella had been left in Lucretia's care, and her absence from the daily prayers, together with Lucretia's odd behavior that evening, left him wondering.

Over the next few nights, Father Francesco observed Lucretia's activities, concealing himself in such a way so that he could better observe without raising her suspicions. And each time, Lucretia's actions were the same: each evening, she would take a scrap of cheese and a wedge of bread, conceal it within the folds of her habit and disappear into the darkness of the hallway, in the opposite direction of the dormitory and of the chapel where evening prayers would soon be held.

One evening, Father Francesco vowed to follow her. Quietly, furtively, hidden in the shadows, he wound his way behind her, walking as softly as he could so as not to attract her attention, concealing himself in unlit crevices, ducking behind darkened archways and obscuring himself in the dim recesses of the gloomy corridors. Soon, he found himself on a familiar path— one that led to the crypts where he had often gone to pray for the dead or to make preparations for those who were about to leave this life. Through the darkness, they made their way, Lucretia walking swiftly, her determined steps and her long, black habit disturbing the dust that had accumulated over the ages, the candle she grasped the only light in that somber chamber, fully unaware that she was being followed, though she stopped, occasionally, to look behind as if she sensed a presence other than her own.

Soon she came to the chamber where Graziella was being held and, through the silence that consumed those eerie catacombs, Father Francesco detected a faint moaning as of a mourner grieving for a loved one or of someone in physical pain. Then, as Sister Lucretia opened the door to that subterranean chamber, there came the slight grating of a chain and the distinct sound of sobbing, and the darkness of the catacombs was cast into an unnatural glow as the light from the torches that burned within flooded the black passageway.

Father Francesco hid behind a crumbling tomb and watched as Sister Lucretia swept into the chamber where Graziella was imprisoned, listened as the sound of Lucretia's voice pierced the silent caverns.

"Here is your meal."

Her words were gruff and her manner even gruffer, and the feeble response that came from my beloved Graziella immediately seized upon Father Francesco's heart.

"I do not wish to eat."

"Do not reject what God has provided. You will partake of what He has given or I shall show you the end of His wrath."

"I do not need sustenance when my fate has been determined."

"You will live until your time comes."

"Why do you keep me like this? Why must you torture me so? Kill me if you must so that I can join God's kingdom, but do not let me languish in his horrible chamber."

Sister Lucretia shoved her severe face into Graziella's and yanked her by her hair.

"Why do you torture me?"

Staring straight into her eyes, Lucretia pondered Graziella's question, then swiftly let her head fall against the stone tomb to which she was chained.

"Because you are evil," she said. "Because God does not take pity on one such as you."

Father Francesco's hands began to tremble as Lucretia's merciless words echoed through the catacombs. It was as if a knife had been suddenly plunged into his soul, for Lucretia's cruelty pained him and Graziella's pitiful responses tore at his very essence. At once, he sank into a cavity of despair and all that he held sacred was put into question. For how, he thought, could one who walked in the shadow of holiness, who professed, through the vows she had taken to uphold *his* hallowed teachings, behave so cruelly? Paralyzed, he crouched behind the cold tomb, and the only response he could muster was to mumble, quietly, to himself a hopeless supplication.

"Whose child is it that are you bearing?"

"I told you. I do not know."

Graziella was crying now such that she could barely pronounce the words that came from her mouth.

"Who is responsible for this? You must confess so that he too can be punished. So that his soul can be cleansed before his death."

"I do not know, I tell you. How many times will you ask? For I will only give the same answer."

"You don't know or you won't say? I will make you confess. And when I am finished, you will beg for His judgment to come as swiftly as the gathering clouds of hell."

A deadly silence followed, broken only by the quiet rustling of Lucretia's habit—a moment in which Father Francesco struggled to make sense of what he was hearing. Sins had been committed. Sins continued. And *his* forgiveness had been forgotten, lost in the shadow of malice and zeal.

And then a loud thud broke into his contemplations as Lucretia began her ministrations, followed by a response so jolting that he could no longer bear to listen, no longer bear to be in the presence of such callousness. Helpless, he squeezed his eyes shut, held back tears of anger and pity and, at last, when he could no longer endure the pain, made a futile sign of the cross, mumbled a useless prayer and rushed swiftly out of those dark passageways, hastened as fast as his footsteps would allow toward the chapel, hurried into that hallowed hall to beg for strength and forgiveness, heedless of the lifeless cadavers that swayed mindlessly in their creaking pews.

Suddenly, he was fully alive, as if his spirit, like the shell of a body that I had rekindled, as if every nerve, every muscle, every inch of his once-dead flesh, was now completely sentient. His soul, once rendered to the tranquil realms of death, now brimmed with the unbearable pangs of life, and the agony he experienced, as he recalled Lucretia's cruel handiwork, refused to dissipate, permeated every inch of his being and burned to his core as if they were the blistering fires of hell.

Ignoring the dull drone that arose from that soulless congregation, he stumbled down the narrow aisle, rushed past pews filled with ashen flesh, and tripped up the steps that led to the altar. Pausing before the tarnished tabernacle, he raised his trembling arms toward the heavens, gazed at the crepe-covered crucifix that was suspended from the gaping apse above and shrank as Lucretia's harsh voice echoed in his head and the sound of Graziella's pleas pierced his wretched soul. Unable now to bear the pain—the realization of who Sister Lucretia truly was—he fell to his knees and cried out in despair.

"Lord! Why do you torture me so!"

His voice echoed through the chapel, hollow in its futility, as the listless assembly stopped their monotonous chanting and stared at him through their hollow eyes. Father Francesco turned toward them, observed them through a cloud of unrelenting anguish as they stood in silence and gazed at him with their lifeless souls.

"Why do you stare at me so? Why do you seek salvation from one such as me when even He does not render it?"

A deadly silence swept through the chapel, broken only by the relentless rustling of vestments as the congregation swayed mindlessly back and forth, waiting for a sign, waiting for someone to tell them what to do or what to say or for leave to return to their icy graves. Father Francesco looked upon them, curious now, as if for the first time he recognized the lack of life beneath their pallid forms, the absence of anything that would constitute a living, sentient being.

I watched, as always, hidden in the shadows. Delighted at the swift transformation in his once resolute eyes— those deep, brown eyes which had once conveyed an aura of steadfastness and calm. Now, all hope had been erased and, in its place, stood the look of a man who had suddenly tasted the reality of life, the reality of the world of mankind—the realization that the horrid acts perpetrated in *his* name were instead committed in mine. Father Francesco was now a man who fully understood the bleakness that had always been there, a bleakness which I, and I alone, had been able to reveal.

Turning once again toward the inverted crucifix, its shapeless form fully confronting him, he reached up in desperation, his fingers plying the air as if attempting to rip off the flimsy crepe that covered it though he could not possibly do so. And then, he raised his trembling voice. Raised it high and loud in sorrow and in pain. But this time it was not prayer that was sung. This time, it was the voice of grief, of torment, of someone whose world had suddenly been shattered and who could no longer bear the lie he had lived for so long.

It was the cry of someone who had suddenly tasted the fiery flames of hell.

Turning toward the congregation, he shouted: "Go! Go and see for yourselves what He has rendered! In the name of God, go and leave me to my misery!"

But his words were only met with silence. Once again, those lifeless figures, obscured by the dim light that filtered into the chapel, stared mutely at him, anxious, confused, restless. Then, having been given the word, they clamored for a way out, looking blindly from one to the other, having perceived a command though what that command meant they could not at all understand. For while Father Francesco's words gave them an inkling of direction—"Go," he continued to shout, "go!"—it was insufficient for their feeble minds to comprehend.

And then, at the back of the room, through the gloomy portal that led from those dark corridors into this sullen, bleak chapel, Lucretia appeared, poised like an apparition emerging from the blackness. Silently she watched, listened as an ominous, baleful sneer broke across her icy face. Slowly, she made her way up the aisle, floating past the congregation, and stared straight ahead at

Father Francesco as her stiff black habit brushed against the wooden pews. Her rosary dangled against her side, and the incessant clicking of bead against bead spawned the only sound that could be heard.

Father Francesco flinched at the sight of her. His despair turned to fear, his fear to horror, as he watched her calmly take her seat at the front of the chapel and motion for her minions to follow. And then, no longer able to bear her stony look, no longer able to endure the uncertainty that had overcome him, he rushed out of the chapel and hurried down the dark corridors of the abbey, lost in a whirl of emotion which he could no longer define.

Chapter 24

Trembling beneath his crumpled cowl, Father Francesco entered his cell and shrank into its bleak austerity. He sought comfort in the relics scattered about the room: the worn bible that stared scornfully from beside his bed; the flimsy breviary, lifeless and mute; the blackened scapular, its obscure face turned to the wall. Objects that now rejected his silent entreaties, trinkets he had worshipped, devoid suddenly of meaning, of solace, of the smallest speck of reassurance.

Numbed by Lucretia's pitiless deeds, his soul reeled in a swirl of confusion and sank into a quagmire from which there seemed no escape. His conscience flared into a seething inferno of doubt and burned a chasm into the bottomless pit of his lifeless existence. Grasping for something with which to steady himself—a spring of soothing water to douse the flames, an anchor to buttress his plummeting soul—he fixed his eyes on the crucifix, suspended above his bed, and cried out in despair to the glum figure whose only answer was a mute stare. Unwilling to accept the reality that he now faced, he grabbed hold of his rosary, fumbled with the twisted strand of wooden beads and bound it tightly around his fingers as he wrestled with the horrors he had witnessed and the pitiless expression on Lucretia's soulless face.

How pitiful to watch a man lose his faith! How wrenching to see one such as Father Francesco grapple with the very fundamentals of doubt! A man who had exuded such conviction, such righteousness, suddenly reduced to a mere shell, brought to his knees—humbled, crushed, cut to the very bones of his faith, a faith that had once kept him erect and sturdy, that had been embedded deep into the flesh of his once sentient life. Having beheld Lucretia's vicious deeds committed in the name of *him* whom they worshipped, having endured, from the shadows of his cowardice, the futile cries and pleas of Graziella as she begged for mercy, his convictions began to crumble, and his belief in the mercy of the heavens came crashing down before him like tiny shards of shattered glass. Surrounded by the rubble of his fate—faced with his own powerlessness to confront evil at its source—he was cut to his aching soul. Reaching out in desperation for consolation, he found none.

I could barely watch him without feeling pity. I was brought to a state that even I, despite my reputation, could not endure—a state of sorrow, of commiseration. Yes, me. The one you have branded as the quintessence of evil. I forced myself to stifle an urge to weep, to refrain from grasping him by the hand, from holding him against my blistered bosom and letting his sorrow—his hot, burning tears—be absorbed into the ashes of my charred flesh.

But I could not succumb to such weakness, for it was I whom he would soon worship. I, who would ultimately be his master. I, to whom he would finally and unquestionably bow. Instead, I allowed him to wallow in his grief, to drown his soul in a well of self-doubt, and I waited for that final moment when he would be disposed to submit to my will.

At last, Father Francesco fell to his knees. He lifted his head in despair, raised his hands—hands that were now lashed together in a twisted coil of useless beads—gaped blankly at the heedless figure on the wall, and lifted his voice in anguish: "Lord! What have I done to deserve your silence?"

Anxiously, he waited—waited for an answer he feared would never come. Waited, hopelessly, for a sign—an indication of any sort—that *his* word—that which had been written through the hands of men, that which he himself had preached to the monks and nuns of the abbey, that which he had staked his entire existence on—might prevail.

"Lord! Will you not answer? Will you not tell me how you allow such malice to infect these holy grounds?"

Receiving no reply, having no clear answer to his pleas, he sank his head into his fettered hands, surrendered, futilely, to his despair, muttered prayers he had memorized from childhood, and emitted a stream of tears that would soften even the most hardened of hearts.

And still he waited. Still the staunch, faithful Father Francesco waited for a reply which he knew in his heart would never come, waited steadfastly, even as his resoluteness began to topple like those useless rosary beads which burst and tumbled, one by one, to the ground as he broke free his shackled hands.

And then, unable to bear it any longer, I intervened. What else could I do? My conscience would not allow me to stand by apathetically.

Silently, I approached him, whispered quietly into his ear, muttered words of comfort, murmured, like the mellifluous purl of a gentle stream, tender hints and soothing suggestions—nothing too rash, nothing too drastic, just enough to salve his throbbing soul, just enough to bring him back from the utter brink of despair. For, after all, he was mine—I had brought him back to life and, like an ungrateful child, he had strayed from my grip as he had done when he was alive. Now, wallowing in a core of misery, in the midst of a life that was both alive and dead, I would claim him, once and for all. He would be in my relentless grip and *he*, once again, would have lost.

A sudden gust of air rushed through the window, stroked Father Francesco's feverish body, tempered the beads of sweat that had broken out on his brow. Outside, the crickets sang their endless song, and a hungry night owl swooped down, searching for its prey. And, through it all, the cry of a lonely wolf rose up as he pursued his hapless mate under the eye of the jaded moon.

Father Francesco rose from his knees, lay down prostrate on his miserable bed, tried to forget, tried to get his mind off the horrors he had witnessed, attempted to dismember the guilt of his cowardice, to ease the vicious bite of his own failure. His thoughts tangled into a twisted coil of remorse and anger, fear and distress, as he battled each one, though he lost every tormented skirmish.

Soon, he became weary and fell into an anxious stupor—a wakeless, tormented daze. His mind brimmed with dreams—dreams of death and destruction, dreams of suffering, of pain and torture. He tossed and turned, tried in vain to rid himself of the ruthless nightmares. Hovering above him, I came to his rescue: instilled in his troubled mind, thoughts more pleasant, infused him with dreams he had not dreamed since the dawn of his awareness. Wild, lustful dreams interrupted only by his muttering attempts at salvation and his trembling body which thrashed back and forth, back and forth—now awake, now in a restless slumber, now in the clutches of twilight sleep. I injected him with every temptation I could, used every trick hidden under my wicked wings to help rid his mind of the horrors he had witnessed, to cure him of his sudden crisis of faith.

Father Francesco resisted as he had resisted all his life, but the more he resisted, the more I endeavored, until my anger at last increased, and the breeze blowing through the window grew into a sudden squall, and the ancient abbey began to tremble in fear. And then, as the rumbling increased, as the abbey shook to its very foundations, as Father Francisco continued to spurn my every advance, he awoke with a start, as the quickening dawn announced its arrival with the cry of a vanquished bird and the hoot of a satiated owl.

Chapter 25

There's a certain beauty in death—one that belies the loathsome existence that came before. Witness the trees that pine in fall—the leaves, once so invariably green, now fading into a pastel of muted tones. The reds and golds. The amber and scarlet. All remnants of what was once living, now quivering, languishing, undulating in the wind as they cling, hopeless, to the barren twigs and branches that once sustained them. The withering remains tumbling, helpless, surrendering to the earth, weaving a lush carpet of foliage fit for a king who, once mighty, lies now deceased. And the deep, deep brown of the soil as it slowly absorbs every fleck of flesh that once was.

So too, Father Francesco—once deep in death, now acutely alive due to my nefarious intercession—tumbling slowly into a gravity of self-doubt: a sentence similar to the one he had arisen from. So too Lucretia, having been spared the soothing hand of death, eternally wandering the corridors of that haunted abbey like a vagrant ghost, restless with the memory of her wicked deeds, struggling between her loyalty to me and her foolish faith in *him*. Unalive to all, even herself. Wishing for death to claim its rightful due, yearning, secretly, to rest, to rest, to rest an everlasting, ever-amnesiac sleep. And so too those other sorry specters, waiting restively in the chapel, who, in life, had gone about their lives like so many untended sheep and who now waited eagerly for someone to steer them, command them, tell them how to act, for they had not the ability to do so on their own.

Yes, death comes in many manifestations!

In that cold chapel, a place so utterly desanctified, those sorry acolytes waited urgently, numbly, unwittingly, for Father Francesco to lead them into salvation; waited for Lucretia to sanction them their evil deeds; waited for me to lure them, whisper into their ears, lead them, guide them to their inevitable destiny, for guidance is the soothing unction for sheer uncertainty. Waited for a sign from *him* that would surely never come!

With a certain glee I observed them—awaiting finality, yearning to return to the grave I had snatched them from, hungering for that silent peace that can only be chiseled by death's artful hand.

And then there was Graziella. Graziella! The one for whom I longed. Languishing in that cold, dark chamber. Bristling with fear and pain. Brimming with cries and tears. Teetering between unconsciousness and weariness. Waiting for that soothing moment when she could at last surrender her life and enter into death's loving arms. *My* arms. For there would be no other to whom she would yield. I would not abide it. For it was I to whom all allegiance would be pledged. *Will* be pledged. Despite what they might think! Despite *his* arrogant desire to the contrary!

At last, the dawn arose—a glorious dawn!—for the sun was burning with vengeance, glaring down upon the remains of an abbey that was once brimming with sanctity. Only now, *his* fields were permanently desiccated, *his* sanctuary fallen into ruin, *his* bell tower in ill-repair, *his* gables damaged, *his* bells cracked and rusted. *His* gardens, once lush with life, now overswept with rot and weed.

It was marvelous to behold. A place once ripe with sanctity, now in the full flourish of my power: a sanctuary, once filled with a semblance of purity—once dedicated to *him*!—alive with the bleak veneer of my iniquity. And I was now in full command!

And Graziella! The prisoner of my soul! Whose turn was soon to come. Who now longed more than ever to join the ranks of the dead. Who, unbeknownst to her innocence, longed for me! Soon, Lucretia would consummate my command and deliver her into my everlasting burning arms. Where she would be forever free. Free to join the grave where so many others had been sent. And Father Francesco, paralyzed, as he was in life, by fear and cowardice, crippled by his inscrutable descent into doubt, would be powerless against my will.

As the dawn began to burn, I summoned Lucretia, aroused her from her meditations, from her silent invocations to *him*. Locked in her room, rosary clasped between her slender fingers, bent on knees in a pose of utmost piety, she endeavored to ignore my command, continued, through her benedictions, to beg for *his* forgiveness, to seek *his* salvation. My heart blackened with envy, throbbed with rage. I stomped my cloven foot and whispered loudly in her ear. Again, she ignored me. Furious, I interrupted her supplications. Enraged, I demanded that she abandon, once and for all, *his* call and remember the pledge she had made to me when she herself had surrendered into the arms of one so young, so fair, so beguiling—surrendered, unbeknownst to her, to me, beneath the halls of that despicable chapel, in that forbidden chamber, surrendered to me in the guise of Father Francesco, heeding my sighs and whispers, succumbing to my irresistible temptations, submitting herself to my will. And then, when the deed was done— when the reality of her weakness rose before her like a charmed snake, it was I who rescued her from ignominy, I who hid the creature, though it was her breast that fed him, her hand that forced him into the shadows, as she craved for forgiveness, begged for protection, pleaded to save her eternally blemished soul. Her life, once so pure, now forever scarred with the dissemblance of her guise and a child whose existence would be forever hidden in the dark shadows of that miserable abbey. After all this, it would be I who would deliver her into the welcoming arms of death once she had performed for me this one last act.

Lucretia flinched at my relentless whispers. Resisting me with every speck of will she could muster, she tightened her grip around those sinuous beads and clutched her bible closely to her breast. Desperate, she reached beneath her bed, for the figure she had hidden there, but my words—unrelenting, burning fiercely like the fires from whence they came—penetrated her soul and refused to abate and, unable to resist any longer, she at last surrendered. Stretching out her emaciated arm, she set that tattered book on her nightstand and relaxed her grip on that twisted string of beads as they dropped helplessly to the ground.

And then she rose, stood up on her withered feet and listened, mesmerized by my hushed murmurings.

"What do you want?"

Her voice, loud and brittle, broke through the silence that hung heavy over that hopeless abbey. Her face, wan and rigid, illuminated by the sunlight which filtered through her open window, stiffened, and her skin rippled with anxiety.

"Why do you torture me so!" she cried.

I did not answer, for there was no need. For what answer can there be to a question that deserves none? That answers itself? When the questioner already knows so well the response? Lucretia knew what I desired, understood quite well why she must obey me, knew that obeisance must overcome whatever loathing she pretended to harbor.

"The girl is there," she said. "Take her and leave me to my suffering."

But I would not abide her self-pity. I would not allow her to abscond from the pledges she had made to me, from the pact she herself had freely made. From the very necessity of obeying me.

"Shall I continue your bidding? Shall I persist in pretending that what I have done—what I do—is in *his* name? I cannot. I shall not any longer!"

And then it was that Lucretia began to pace the room. *Sister* Lucretia. Like an animal whose only desire was to find escape, to survive, to follow an instinct whose very meaning was as clear as the dawn to which it had awakened. Stopping before the cross where *his* image had once hung, she folded her trembling hands in prayer, struggled as her face turned red with desperation, as the tears burned her flesh, as her nostrils flared with the incomprehensible knowledge of all the evil deeds she had committed.

But I could not tolerate her childish protests, and I continued to whisper in her ear, longer and louder until the thought of salvation—the thought of *him*—could no longer be heeded.

"Why do you torture me so!" she cried yet again.

Lucretia fell to her knees, fell into a spasm of despair. She pounded her hand against her breast, pulled at her hair, folded her hands tightly around her torso, abandoned herself into shudders of fear and loathing. And through it all, I sustained my whispers, continued to lure her into the trap she had made for herself, persisted in reminding her of her obligation to me. Until the buzzing I conjured in her head could no longer be endured. Until her face twisted into a grimace that mirrored the soul that I had helped to mold.

I did nothing further. There was no need. For Lucretia's soul burned with a fire that I no longer needed to stoke. She stood and, with a sudden leap, with a cry that echoed through the hallways of the abbey, rushed out of her pestilent cell, ran toward the place where her fate would be sealed with the fulfillment of a wish I no longer had need to speak.

Chapter 26

The sunlight filtered bleakly through the slivered stained glass, penetrated the dark, hazy atmosphere, roiling with flies and flecks of dead skin, onto the pallid faces of a condemned congregation who waited impatiently in the stillness of that stricken chapel. The dull buzz of their muted voices filled the church like a drone of wasps, and the vacant look on their lifeless faces mirrored the cold emptiness of the abbey and the fiery abyss of their barren souls, souls that had been abandoned to the underworld from which they had recently been snatched.

How marvelous to see them! How splendid to observe them in that blighted environment! To behold the culmination of my contrivance! How elated I felt then to witness my sinister arrangement—to feast on the destruction of *his* design, a design that had been rendered so carefully and from which I had been unjustly banished. Here was the climax of an eternity of hatred and acrimony for having been singled out, for having been struck down and cast into a realm of disillusionment. Here, in *his* universe, here in this sanctuary meant to mirror *his* design, was the architecture of my revenge, the culmination of a battle in which I could at last claim victory.

There they stood. Groveling in their misery. Languishing in a world of inertia and uncertainty. Yearning for the soothing caress of death from which they had come when it was the very life *he* had bestowed upon them they should have been craving. I watched them enshrouded in the rubble of that doomed chapel, burrowed amidst the broken beams and shattered glass where any façade of tranquility, of bliss, of comfort, had been replaced by the dissemblance of flaking walls and crooked floors, of crumbling ceilings, of pews and kneelers so damaged they could no longer sustain those who knelt upon them. It was the total destruction of *his* universe in which I now rejoiced!

And yet, I wanted more. I wanted to possess each and every one of them, to own them, to claim them as mine. I wanted them to bow to me, to worship me, to pledge their eternal allegiance to me. I wanted them to recognize *me* as the sole being to whom they must vow obeisance!

And then—And then!

And then, Sister Lucretia rushed into the chapel. Lucretia, that marvelous creature who had given no short shrift to my wishes, though she struggled with her profession of loyalty, though she resisted, in vain, her desire to surrender to me—Sister Lucretia swooped in, ready to do my final bidding. Her veil fluttered in her wake as if she were transported by the wind; her black habit rustled as she swept menacingly past those numb specters in that morbid congregation.

And then she stopped. Stopped at the head of that gruesome assembly. The chapel was still and silent, as if all semblance of life had been sucked from it, and Lucretia stood in front of that lost flock of lifeless mendicants and eyed them each with the voracity of a vulture. Savored each one of them with her glaring eye as if they were there for her sustenance. And they looked at her, possessed by her presence, ignited by the fire that flared in that wicked eye, relieved that here, at last, was someone who had come to lead them, someone who would finally give purpose to their frail lives.

No word was said, for none was needed. For it was her malicious eye that spoke. That burning orb—black as coal, wild like a blinding inferno, glistening with the temptation of a soothing poison. And they all knew—understood as she gazed with vehemence at their miserable faces, as she stared mendaciously into their empty souls—they understood, instinctively, that they would follow—knew, all too well, that now was the time they would act to still their wretched souls.

Swiftly, they stirred. Fiercely. Mesmerized, they filed out from those broken pews, ready to abandon that illusive chapel, and lined up, one by one, before Sister Lucretia, ready to obey even her most evil command.

And then she reached for her rosary, extended her withered arm, grabbed the dangling crucifix with her bony fingers and raised it up into the air, ripped the glum figure from its wooden resting place and wielded it before them, holding it up for all to see until, at last, she dropped it onto the floor and crushed it with the heel of her shriveled foot. And their eyes lit up like fire. And their faces, devoid of emotion, swelled with fervor. And their voices rose into a fervent cacophony of vengeance.

And then it was that Lucretia—*my* protégé—flush with zeal, fully relinquished at last, made her move, marched to the rear of the chapel, resolute in her loyalty to me, a lieutenant in an army of evil. And they followed, followed like the deathly demons that they were, prepared for the final climax of their barren lives.

Chapter 27

A woeful wind moaned for the dead souls trapped inside that unsanctified abbey and lashed through Father Francesco's listless cell. An icy chill swaddled him like a winding sheet, and he squirmed through its frosty folds as if resisting a heavy pall. Trapped inside its relentless grip, he sought comfort in the vague veils of sleep as the sound of the midnight bell clanged bitterly from its crumbling belfry and ceased its baleful litany upon the eleventh stroke.

Father Francesco awoke with a start. A full moon glared through the broken windowpane. Dazed, he stared at the spent candle on his night table, heedless of the shadows assembling upon his barren walls.

Soon, a faint howling arose as the weary ghosts of the abbey materialized, their teeth gnashing, their bones grinding, their eyes brimming with terror. Fallen souls, they were lost to eternity, trapped in a maelstrom of misery. Unleashed from the catacombs, they came demanding intercession and cried out to that diffident monk for his refusal to save them from eternal damnation. It was a cacophony of evil, a grotesque choir of the damned—moaning and shrieking, seeking deliverance from *his* everlasting judgment, congregating in a cell whose occupant was neither dead nor alive.

Father Francesco shrank into his bed. He covered his eyes with the flimsy shroud that shielded him, but the ghosts seized him with their rotten limbs and refused to release their grip. He closed his eyes, but the calloused veil of flesh was not enough to blind him against their presence, and the shrill cries of agony echoed across eternity and filled him with dread.

Merciless, the damned surrounded him. Arisen from their graves, freed from the sting of conscience, they sought retribution. Unfettered, they struck out and demanded redemption, but Father Francesco dismissed their pleas as he had done when they were alive. Instead, he quickened beneath his useless armor. His cold limbs stirred as his soul awakened. Gazing at the broken bones and fangless grins that filled him with horror, he witnessed what his eyes had long denied, unfolding now beneath the inky night, beneath the glaring eye of the merciless moon, unveiling the disillusion he had always denied. For beneath the naked light, the sinners revealed their sins, as vivid as the dead fingers with which he covered his face, and repeated their crimes as their victims succumbed. He watched the horrors unfold with eyes bare of the blindness he had fostered when he was alive, and he understood that he could no longer ignore the transgressions he had buried deep within the bowels of that heartless abbey.

The guilty gaped at him with their hideous grins. Pitiless, they reenacted their deeds for him to see as they mourned the loss of their souls. For like me, they had been condemned to an eternity of misery, and their shrill cries for mercy went unheard just as mine had.

What a spectacle it was! How I reveled in its incarnation as Father Francesco cowered at each revelation. But even now, he refused to acknowledge the supremacy of evil in a world of depraved men and women—a world which had been carefully cloaked in all *his* flimsy array!

I howled with joy. A strident, growling bellow emerged from deep within my bloated belly. It manifested itself in the relentless wind raging outside Father Francesco's shattered window and infused the cries of those who had stumbled my way with an unquenchable fear. For they would always suffer as *he* had meant them to. And now it was that false monk's turn to surrender, for no man, dead or alive, can escape their rightful destiny.

Father Francesco turned. Suddenly, he understood something he had long refused to acknowledge. A truth that had been hidden all his life. For through the bluster of misery that raged before his eyes, there arose a faint cry. A cry which penetrated the thick layer of cowardice that encased Father Francesco's soul and leached through the brilliant luster he had deceived himself with all his life.

Immediately, he knew who it was. Knew, without question, what was her plight as intimately as he knew the book he had revered, knew what he must do as he knew so well the verses he had read till reading was no longer needed. And he trembled from the fear of it. And he trembled from the very thought that her life—her salvation—was solely in his hands.

He tried to ignore it, prayed it would dissipate into the wind. But the cries resisted his prayers and refused to abide by his pleas. Invoking *his* name, he gathered up his strength—gathered it as one gathers the bones of the dead—and rushed out of that haunted room, rushed through the halls of misery, grasping the candle, which I brought suddenly to life. Cupping his fingers around the meager flame, he hurried through the courtyard, vacant now of all the souls whose lives had been lost, and made his way down the stone steps that led to the ancient crypts and beyond.

Chapter 28

As the fiendish winds blew with wrath and the feeble flame surrendered its pitiful grip on life, Father Francesco stumbled through the murky bowels of that unforgiving abbey. Staggering through the web of tunnels, he drifted past the twisted corpses that had returned to their resting place.

Cries of torment echoed through the musty catacombs and summoned him further toward his fate while faint whispers reverberated through his head, urging him to return to his cell where he could cradle *his* book and seek the delusive comfort of prayer. But his body moved forward without heed as if it had been cut off from the very source of life.

And I, with a jaundiced eye, lit his way. I guided him through a maze of narrow passageways, enticing him as he pleaded with *him* and strove to deflect my advances. But I am not one to give up, and so I persisted as I have done throughout the ages. I nursed his uncertainties and seduced his soul as it churned with the revelation of his incertitude. I watched with glee as he wavered between loyalty to *him* and the unspoken knowledge that I would prevail. And all the while, I charmed him, whispered gently in his ear. I sowed doubt, aroused resistance, tempted him with guilelessness, confused him with quandaries no man could resolve. And yet, he persisted in shirking my advances, insisted on invoking *his* name and mumbling empty prayers until, surrendering to the inevitable, he approached the entrance to the forbidden chamber he had long denied.

Breathing in the foulness that surrounded him and raising his eyes to the invisible heavens, he thrust his hand inside his pocket and snatched the ring of keys he had no wish to grasp. Trembling, he swung the door open and came face to face with what he had no wish to see.

"Vile woman! Let the evil pass from your wicked flesh!"

The light from the burning torches filled Lucretia's stark silhouette with their hellish glow. Her stiff black habit scraped against Graziella's swollen face. Hovering like a vulture, she commanded her acolytes who obeyed her every demand. Shackled to the stone tomb where she would finally rest, Graziella cried out as the pangs of birth and the sting of Lucretia's torture increased.

"Peace be upon you, Father."

Lucretia planted her evil eye on Father Francesco's pale face. He gazed upon her with a clarity he had not known as the wrinkles on her shriveled visage began to swell and the Mother Superior he had known for so long disappeared. And then he turned to Graziella—poor Graziella, *my* Graziella—and watched in horror as those mindless nuns, swarming like a ring of black spiders, obeyed Lucretia's malicious bidding.

"In the name of God, Sister Lucretia! What is the meaning of this?"

"We are helping this unfortunate woman through her trial, Father," she replied.

She clenched her lips over her toothless jaws as her evil eye flared with its sulfurous glow.

"Sister Lucretia. I will not—"

But just then, Graziella let out a cry as those soulless nuns pinned her down to the tomb she would soon enter.

"We are handling this as God commands," Lucretia said.

"God does not command such cruelty!"

Clutching the string of beads by her side with her bony fingers, she took one step toward Father Francisco and pierced him with a look that made him shrink. Then, she gripped the cross, bare of its victim, and squeezed it until that wretched eye seemed to burst from its very socket. Raising it like a weapon, she pointed it at Father Francesco and said: "I am in command here now. I am doing what you have neglected to do. More hot water!"

"Let me be, in God's name!"

"In God's name, woman!? Do you now call on God when you have abandoned Him? Do you now call on God when you have neglected His commands and fallen into disrepute? You should have prayed for His guidance before you committed your wicked deed. You must let the child out so that we can destroy it and you can be purged of your sins."

"You cannot!"

A wave of contractions overcame Graziella's protests as the unborn child quickened its entry into a world it would soon regret. Lucretia yanked her by her long, sweaty hair and shoved her stringent face into hers.

"It is evil," she whispered. "Like you. Like its father. Tell me who he is for he too must be punished. We cannot let these acts stain the walls of our sacred dwelling!"

"You cannot," Graziella repeated.

"You have no choice."

Graziella's head crashed against the stone tomb as Lucretia released her grip. Her face twisted in agony and her body thrashed from side to side. And the child—the innocent child—inched its way into a world that would soon sniff out its budding life.

"Sister Lucretia. I will not allow you to defile the abbey in this way."

"Defile? Defile, Father Francesco?"

She curled her lips up in derision.

"Am I to understand that you condone this woman's behavior?"

"I demand that you show mercy!"

She stared at Father Francesco, stared until the hairs on his back rose and the courage he had mustered began to sink.

"Very well," she answered.

Lucretia watched Father Francesco shrink into his flimsy cowl. She looked around the chamber and stared as those mindless zombies attacked Graziella with zeal. And then, looking down to the corridors of hell—looking at me—her skin erupted and from each pore of her rotten skin, maggots emerged crawling out of their fetid birthplace and consuming every inch of her breathless body.

"Bring the hot oil," she hollered. "Boiling, scalding oil."

Father Francesco trembled. He could not talk, could not pronounce the words that had been implanted in his soul. Instead, he looked from Lucretia to Graziella to the coterie of nuns who were oblivious to the world. Helpless, he rushed out of that unholy chamber, rushed toward his grave and to an eternity where uncertainty would forever rule.

I tried my best to save him. Reminded him of his sacred duties. His calling. Of the vows he had made to *him*. Tried to instill a bit of conviction into that shallow shell. But he would not listen. He would not heed the words he had long refused to hear. And so he abandoned Graziella whose very salvation was his charge, relinquished all responsibility and left her to the wiles of Lucretia—my protégé, the one I had succeeded in creating in my image.

It was then that the wicked winds infiltrated the dank corridors of those sorry catacombs. The torches flickered helplessly but could not sustain their light and, at last, they were quenched, leaving Lucretia and her clutch of nuns in total darkness. Invoking *his* name and clutching the beads that swayed by their sides, they hastened to flee out of that cruel chamber to the narrow passageways of salvation, guided only by a thin sliver of light cutting its way through the dank catacombs.

And then, as they rushed away toward safety, that boiling cauldron of oil, which Lucretia had intended for Graziella—the woman who was now without question, mine—tipped over, spilling its fiery contents into the musty corridors and engulfing those sorry souls in its burning hunger.

Chapter 29

I don't need to go on any further, do I? You know the ending just well as I do, just as you know what will happen next. It's in your heart. It's in every ounce of your wretched soul. For I've told you a story you know very well. Deep, deep down in the depths of your very existence.

Or, perhaps, it's you who's telling me.

As for me, I've exposed my burning heart to you. You know now what my motivations were. Who I loved and who I hated and all that comes in between. And perhaps, now you know a little more about yourself. More than you ever wished to. Perhaps, you sympathize with me. Like me, even. Appreciate my dilemma. After all, I'm not all that bad. At least, not as bad as they've made me out to be. Not so bad that you might not let me sneak into your heart at times. Knowingly. Willingly. Without resistance.

For, like you, I was created in *his* image. Only, I was cast away. For a mere grievance. A simple misunderstanding. Just because I wanted to be loved and adored.

Like we all do. Just because I was the most beautiful of all the angels. Now I ask you: Was that fair? Why should I have to live a life of misery just because of the way I was created! I mean, *he* made me as he saw fit. Am I then just a scapegoat? The sacrificial lamb? The scale on which all good and evil is to be judged? All because of *his* scheme? Why did it have to be me? That's all I'm asking. And have I received an answer? Will you ever receive an answer?

You walk around in your arrogance, an arrogance disguised as humility. Unscathed. Pretending to ignore me. Endeavoring, with all your self-righteous might, to resist me at every turn. Trying to rid yourself of me when, deep down, you know that you have the same capacity for evil as I. Is there not, after all, a part of me in you, just as there is a part of you in me? Are you not complicit? Do you not condone *his* ignominious deed while refusing to acknowledge what you have done in my name? In your every action, day in and day out, as you curse my existence, as you spurn me at every turn—do you not see how unfair, how hypocritical, you are when you have been commanded to show mercy, forgive others, to exhibit even one crumb of kindness? To turn the other cheek? I am, in the end, just another poor soul who you heartlessly cast aside as you go about your business, ignoring *his* decrees.

So now you've heard my story—the story of me and Graziella. A story of love. *My* love. Ah yes, perhaps she was unaware. But then, aren't we all? Who is to say out loud what one thinks, what one desires, what one hides in the secret depths of their sorry souls? Who is to believe the façade we present every day? Are we not, in the end, all entombed in the same miserable circumstances?

Do you understand me now? Can you trust me? Just a little? Enough for you to take my side? Just once? Just for a tiny bit?

After all, I have a very warm heart.

Acknowledgements

This book is a result of my passion for gothic novels, and so I owe much debt to those who showed the way: Horace Walpole, Ann Radcliffe, Charles Maturin, Bram Stoker, Mikhail Bulgakov and Mary Shelley. When I was an undergraduate student at Queens College (CUNY), I was lucky enough to take a course in the gothic novel. This fed into interests already nascent. And so my thanks go to those professors I had way back who helped stimulate my interests and my imagination.

I also want to thank Jessica Bell and all those at Vine Leaves Press who have believed in me from the beginning. If it weren't for them, my fiction, curious as it is, would not have seen the light of day.

And to my wife, who has given me the space to practice my madness, and to my children, to whom I leave a legacy of words.

Vine Leaves Press

Enjoyed this book?
Go to *vineleavespress.com* to find more.
Subscribe to our newsletter: